A NOVEL

ROBERT GUSSIN

Oceanview Publishing

IPSWICH, MASSACHUSETTS

Illustrations by Melissa Stewart

ISBN-10: 1-933515-04-X
ISBN-13: 978-1-933515-04-5

Published in the United States by Oceanview Publishing,
Ipswich, Massachuetts
Visit our Web site at oceanviewpub.com
Distributed by Midpoint Trade Books
www.midpointtradebooks.com

10 9 8 7 6 5 4 3 2 1

PRINTED IN THE UNITED STATES OF AMERICA

This book is dedicated to my wife, Pat,
and our children, Jeff, Bill, Lisa, Joe,
Lynne, Wayne, and Ben.
They are a constant inspiration.

Florida novelists have a special talent when it comes to infusing humor into stories about serious topics, especially the environment. Two of the best are Carl Hiaasen and Tim Dorsey. It was their work that inspired me to write *Trash Talk*.

I want to thank all my friends and family who made me a huge sports enthusiast — more like a fanatic. That's why *Trash Talk* is about professional athletes.

And a special thanks to my ganddaughter, Melissa Stewart, for the illustrations. Not only is Melissa a talented artist, but she's a medical student as well.

And finally, I want to thank my wife, Pat, for encouraging me to start writing this book and then for her continuous prodding to finish it. Without her this book would not have happened nor would have any of the other wonderful things in my life. I can never thank her enough.

Maxwell Gordon was having a bad day. The six foot eleven, 250-pound center for the Orlando Stars was pissed off at David Kress, Commissioner of the National Basketball Association and at Whitey Starzl, that little shit, skinny-ass guard for the Streaks. Not only had Philadelphia beaten the Stars on the previous evening, but the six foot five, 200-pound Starzl had peppered Gordon with so many insults, culminating with one about his mother, that Gordon had taken a wild swing at Starzl, which cost him a two-game suspension and a $10,000 fine. If I had only hit the little bastard,

Gordon thought, I would have knocked him into the stands.

Now, Gordon had this additional shit in the letter from Commissioner Kress. The Commissioner, in his infinite wisdom, had decided that it was time to add a little culture to his players, and class to the league. So, starting immediately, every player in the league had to attend at least one meeting or "symposium" — educational in nature — per year. Naturally, their teams would pay all fees and travel expenses. These had to be legitimate offerings, and at least one day long. What a bunch of crap, Gordon thought. Why the hell does Kress think I went to college? Just to play basketball? Shit, thirty more credits and I can get my degree. I'm sure Michigan State will take me back in a few years after I make a little money. And these fuckin' courses got to be taken in the off-season. Bullshit!

Arnie Schwartz was more excited than he had been since his Bar Mitzvah, and he was now thirty-two-years-old. Seven years working for the Sarasota Environmentalist Society, and they were giving him the responsibility to set up the Annual National Environmentalist Meeting to be held in Sarasota this year for the first time since 1957. Even the advertisements and other promotional material would be his to plan. If only they had decided that he would be "the man" earlier. With only five months until the May meeting, the pressure was on Arnie.

Arnie was not particularly adept at working

under pressure. At five foot four and 170 pounds, he was a bit rotund, and tended to move about rather slowly. His thick glasses and pudginess gave him a scholarly appearance. Since his graduation from Rutgers, Arnie had been working for the Sarasota Environmentalist organization. Although he loved the job, it took Arnie more than a year in Sarasota to become comfortable living alone and in a new area of the country. Arnie grew up in East Brunswick, New Jersey, and lived with his parents until he graduated from college and was hired by the Sarasota group. He even passed up the opportunity to live in the dormitory at college, and chose to stay at home and commute to school. When he moved to Sarasota, he decorated his small apartment to look like his former room in his parents' home.

Even Arnie considered himself sort of nerdy, and rarely dated, or in fact, went out with anyone — even the guys — socially. He did go to the YMCA once or twice a week to play chess or checkers, which, along with television, was his favorite pastime. Arnie had gone to one of the spring training baseball games in Sarasota with a neighbor in the apartment house, but had not cared much for it. He just never became enamored with sports the way many of his college classmates did. But his grades were reasonably good, and he landed the Sarasota job fairly quickly after graduation.

Arnie had always been kind and good-hearted and, when he wanted to, could make friends fairly easily. He was very much liked by his neighbors, particularly those on the elderly side, because he often carried in their groceries, carried out their garbage, and even, on occasion, washed their cars.

But now Arnie dived into action with a passion not before seen in the Sarasota Environmentalist Society office. Within a week he had set aside one hundred rooms at the Sarasota Hyatt and had reserved the grand ballroom and six meeting rooms that would hold about fifty people each. He reserved the ballroom for daytime meetings and for two evenings for special occasions that he envisioned would take place during the four-day meeting. Arnie's mind was going a mile a minute. Participants would arrive on Sunday evening to a welcoming reception. Monday, Tuesday, Wednesday, and Thursday would provide a mixture of large plenary sessions to address major topics plus smaller specialty sessions and workshops.

Arnie recruited three of the remaining eight employees of the Sarasota office as his team. They were Melissa Stanford, the office secretary; Jordan (Jordy) Gifford, the public relations specialist; and

Pamela Swain, whose main job was to organize demonstrations and protests when local environmental issues warranted it.

The director of the office, Rama Schriff, was impressed with Arnie's enthusiasm and energy. Mr. Schriff had emigrated to Sarasota from Calcutta (now Kolkata), India, only eight years prior, and had a bit of difficulty appreciating the seriousness of any of Sarasota's environmental issues. But the pay was adequate, and Mr. Schriff had reasonable management skills and a background of having dealt with some fascinating environmental problems back in Calcutta.

What had clinched the job for Mr. Schriff when he interviewed with the Board in Sarasota was how he'd significantly reduced air pollution and smog in Calcutta. Schriff was working as a chemist in the city lab when he became interested in the smog problem. He decided to explore the major culprits contributing to the pollution, smog, and resultant poor air quality. Schriff was dogged in his pursuit. He analyzed garbage he found on the streets, polluting emissions from vehicles, and smoke from cooking fires. But the breakthrough came when he analyzed a sample of dung from the sacred cows that wandered freely on the streets of Calcutta. To Schriff's surprise, the dung was loaded with volatile, air-polluting substances.

Schriff was shocked and fascinated. So as not to offend any of his fellow citizens, he went out at night with special collection containers and collected gases from both ends of the sacred animals as well as more dung. He found all of his samples to be highly polluting. Schriff calculated that each cow emitted almost twenty pounds of pollutants a year as gases from manure, regurgitation, and flatulence.

What touched a sensitive chord with the Board of the Sarasota Environmentalist Society was the way Schriff handled this delicate issue. He requested meetings with his supervisor and then with the city leaders. He apprised them of his findings in very private meetings and then suggested that if they could very subtly move the sacred animals to a "sacred pasture" outside the city, the smog problem should dissipate. The city fathers admired the young man's intellect and courage and accepted his advice.

The cows were slowly and quietly guided over time to a site just outside the city. Although the mass of citizens never realized what happened, they all appreciated the sudden decrease in smog and increase in air quality. The newly visible sunshine was accepted as a blessing by all.

Rama Schriff was promoted to a director in the Office of Environmental Issues and then, two years later, was discovered by the Sarasota group shortly after he and his family decided to seek a different lifestyle and moved to Florida.

Schriff had melded into the Florida group quite well. His managerial style was very passive and he allowed his people to do their jobs without much input from him. Sometimes the group wished he were more involved. True to form, he was supportive of the planning committee, but did not contribute significantly to the process.

Once Arnie and his team had the meeting location and hotel rooms set, they began to think about the major theme for the meeting so that they could begin to plan a program and invite speakers. They also would have to put out a call for abstracts of presentations to be given in different sessions by members of the National Environmentalist Society, students, and other attendees who wished to present.

"Well guys, what do you think?" Arnie asked at the first meeting of his small committee at which they were addressing theme and program.

"I think the theme should be global warming," said Pam. "It will screw up our ocean temperature and kill the fish and ruin our tourist industry here, as well as endanger the food supply nationally and globally.

"I don't think so," said Jordy. "We don't even

see agreement as to whether there is global warming or global cooling."

"Well," said Pam, "we could do both. You know, what are the long-term effects of global warming or global cooling?"

Melissa chimed in. "I believe that the biggest problem today is trash. We are generating so damned much of it, and we have no place to put it. Everybody has the 'not in my backyard' syndrome."

"I like that." said Arnie. "Trash really is a big problem, and it's everyone's problem everywhere. All the members should have an interest."

"Yeah, that's right," said Jordy, "but it doesn't sound like a topic that's going to excite our membership. 'Come and make a presentation on trash.' Not much pizzazz in that!"

"Hey, trash talk can be exciting," Melissa said.

"Hell," cried Arnie. "That's it. Trash talk. Melissa, you're a genius. Jordy, why didn't you think of that? That's really a catchy name. Short and to the point. What a great title for our conference. I love it. 'Trash Talk.' It's a great major theme, and will lead to all kinds of interesting sessions on biodegradability, incineration, waste hauling, dump sites, and so forth. Hell guys, this is going to be the best Environmentalist meeting ever!"

The joy and excitement that filled the little conference room was palpable. Jordy ran down the hall and came back with a flip chart on an easel and a handful of Magic Markers.

Pam was practically jumping up and down helping Jordy set up the easel. "I can't wait to design some posters," she said. "It will be great to put together a poster that's not urging people to fight some environment-harming issue."

Pam's job setting up demonstrations usually involved attacking a major corporation for polluting or a local politician for supporting legislation that might lead to environmental damage. Pam was involved in protest-type activities during high school in Orlando, where she grew up. She continued the battles through her days at the University of Florida, while majoring in political science. Pam felt that she was born too late, for she considered the Vietnam War era to have been the Holy Grail for protestors. She dreamed of being knocked down and kicked by a Chicago policeman or tear-gassed in Philadelphia or clubbed by a Columbus, Ohio cop.

Now she had to settle for the milder battles of south central Florida. Last month she led a protest against the residents of several large oceanfront condominiums for keeping porch lights on during the sea turtle hatching season. The belief is that the emerging baby turtles turn toward the lights, and go away from rather than into the ocean. This is the popular belief, but there have been few, if any, reports of infant sea turtles scratching on the doors of condominium owners.

Pam had also led a protest against a group responsible for transporting alligators from residential properties to swamp areas. Although these wandering alligators are responsible for the disappearance of numerous small dogs and cats, much to the horror of the pet owners, Pam and her colleagues believe that the land belongs to the wild animals and that humans and their unfortunate pets are the trespassers.

But now Pam could put her energy to a use that would influence far more people on a national, and perhaps even an international scale. How great that would be!

Melissa was still seated at the conference table staring into space. She was elated that this group had embraced her theme. She was thinking of her role in setting up the entertainment. She knew that she would have to test some restaurants to assure that they would be appropriate to recommend to the participants. On her secretary's salary, she didn't get to eat out very often, except for an occasional stop at McDonald's or Wendy's. Her money was going toward night school tuition at the local campus of the University of South Florida, where Melissa was about twenty-six credits short of a degree in journalism. If she continued on Wednesday evenings and Saturday mornings, she figured another two years until she would graduate. Melissa lived at home with her parents and so her other expenses were minimal. She loved her job at the Society. She hoped after she had her degree, she could stay on with more responsibility and a larger salary. But for now she was so excited about the national meeting opportunity, everything else seemed secondary.

Max Gordon was bitching about his woes to everyone he could— in person or on the phone. He
called his best friend in the league, Moe Robbins,
who played for Dallas.

"The fucker gave me a two-game suspension
and fined me 10,000 bucks, and I never even
touched that son of a bitch Starzyl. Christ, if I had
hit him, I probably would be suspended for fifty
years! And this shit about going to courses or
meetings. Holy fuck. Did you get that letter?"

"You bet your ass I did," said Moe, "and so did
all my teammates, and I'm sure all of us in the
league. Even worse, my buddies from the Cowboys

got it. So it's some kind of conspiracy by those dick-head commissioners of all the pro sports to turn us into some kind of pansy ass, ballet dancin', sissy shits. Pretty soon they'll be requirin' us to go to the opera and read fuckin' historical novels."

"You're shittin' me, Moe. The football guys got to do it too?" Max asked.

"No shit, just like us," said Moe.

"Hey, Moe, why don't you ask your Cowboy buddy Tony DiMarco, where he's gonna drag his 385 pound ass. The seats at the ballet are too little to hold him. They're made for those little round lady asses and the bony butts of those 'in-tell-a-gensia' men."

"Hey, brother," Moe said, "keep me informed of your choices. Maybe we can learn together."

They were both roaring with laughter when they hung up.

The news of the commissioners' directive spread like wildfire through the sports community. There was even talk that baseball players, the intellectual elite of the sports world, might get the same requirements, and hockey players too. It rained like a plague down on the athletes. Every sports columnist wrote about it. Cartoonists portrayed huge football players in full uniform with a mortarboard replacing their helmet. Basketball cartoonists showed what looked like seven-footers dunking an encyclopedia through the basket. One cartoon showed a baseball player showing a hockey player some lines in a book by Shakespeare, while two hockey players on skates, but with tutus replacing their uniforms, practiced at a ballet bar.

The conference planning team in Sarasota was working feverishly. Pamela was on the phone to well-known specialists from around the nation requesting they arrange symposia on important topics related to trash. Sue Greber from Harvard had agreed to handle a symposium on recreational trash. Sonje Bhat from Princeton agreed to a biodegradability session. Professor Jacques Dimone from the University of British Columbia said his work, which showed that some weed killers could cause male frogs to develop multiple sex organs, would be a great plenary session major presentation. Pam agreed. Dale Bowl from the University of Florida, an expert on fish, agreed to talk about the impact of red tide on the fish population, and the problems of dead fish disposal.

Pam was certain that the way things were moving, filling a program with exciting, interesting, educational presentations was going to be easy.

Jordy Gifford was thrilled to have the advertising and publicity assignment. Even though the title was not his idea, he had grown to really like it and appreciate its potential to lure a broad audience to the meeting. Jordy's mind was going a mile a minute. Not only would he run ads in the environmental publications, but he thought this conference could attract a broader audience and get more people involved in the environmental movement. He planned to even place some ads in the general news media. Jordy was now fulfilling one of his dreams. He was actually designing an ad campaign. On a picture of an overloaded garbage can with bottles, cans, and other assorted items protruding in a mound above the top of the can, Jordy had printed in large letters: TRASH TALK.

The words formed a sort of semi-circle on the side of the can, the roundness of the can distorting the words into the slightly circular appearance. Below the can, the advertising copy read: "This is your opportunity to participate in 'Trash Talk.' A chance to learn from the experts and discuss your ideas. What's in our future? Come to Sarasota, Florida, May 27–May 31. For more information contact: Jordan Gifford, 1218 Lime Street, Sarasota, Florida 34280 or call 1-800-668-7274.

Jordy was like a kid in a candy store. The five foot nine blond with blue eyes looked like the stereotypical California surfer. In fact, Jordy had grown up in San Diego, where his father owned a very successful advertising agency. Jordy's dream, as well as his father's, was for Jordy to follow in his footsteps and eventually take over the advertising agency. However, it did not take long in young Jordy's life to realize that the talent and the drive were lacking. His dad ultimately, and with great difficulty, accepted the fact that Jordy would never be his successor in the business. Jordy accepted that much earlier than his father, but he still hoped to enter the advertising business in some role.

The job with the Sarasota Environmentalist Society had been a godsend. Jordy met a girl while on a post-college graduation vacation to Florida, who listened to Jordy bemoan his future and express his career desires. She alerted him to a possibility that she had heard about from a friend in Sarasota. Almost miraculously, after a telephone discussion about Jordy's journalism major in college and his general knowledge of advertising due to his father's influence, Jordy had an interview and was offered the role of public relations manager. He was also asked to handle whatever minor advertising the group might require.

He became Rama Schriff's first hire shortly after Schriff had arrived some four years earlier. The job level and requirements seemed to suit Jordy's limited talents quite well and, even though at times he did display a bit of undeserved arrogance, he fit in well with the rest of the group.

The national meeting was Jordy's dream. It was like his greatest wish came true, a real advertising campaign. He was even able to overcome the disappointment of having less time to sail his small sailboat in Sarasota Bay, which had replaced his so-so surfing as his only physical activity since he arrived in Sarasota.

Melissa and Arnie were exploring opportunities for social events during the meeting. Sarasota in May, Arnie thought. What a beautiful time. Melissa suggested large sailboat cruises around the bay and even into the gulf. The attendees would appreciate the idea of minimal use of motors and minimal pollution compared to the large sightseeing yachts that regularly navigated the waters. Arnie thought of guided walks to the art galleries on Palm Avenue and perhaps a performance at the Van Wezel Performing Arts Center. Melissa agreed to find out what was on the program for the end of May.

"And no one should come to Sarasota without a visit to the Ringling Museum and Cor d'Zan, the newly renovated home of John and Mable Ringling, the circus founders."

"So much to do and so little time," Arnie chirped as he practically pranced around the office. His state of excitement had not dissipated in the weeks since he received this assignment. Life was good for Arnie Schwartz.

The community of professional athletes couldn't believe the curse that had befallen them. What could those jackass commissioners be thinking?

Meanwhile the 'jackass' commissioners had their own take on the situation. They were on the phone to each other as much as were the players. They were elated with the outcome of their historic meeting.

Bert Salen, the baseball commissioner, called Kress the day after the meeting. "David, that was a fabulous suggestion you made about additional education. You're a genius."

"Thanks, Bert, but it was really a joint effort.

Phil's idea to require continuing education on an annual basis was really the clincher. He's had more than his share of problems with the football players. Hell, maybe our players will learn how to put sentences together."

"Yeah," Salen responded. "Remember the interview with Randy Matson two weeks ago? The only thing understandable was when he said that line drive hit him in the balls. It would have caused him a lot less damage if it had hit him in the head." Salen continued, "I was also really pleased with Bitten's participation and willingness to go along with the idea. His hockey players don't get interviewed that often so they have less chance to look like idiots."

"That's true," said Kress, "but they've had plenty of problems too. A few weeks ago Serge Kikamin from Boston broke a guy's jaw in the parking lot after a game because the guy told him that he should be sent back to the minors."

"Oh yeah," agreed Salen, "and there was that fight between the Red Wings and the group of people in the seats. Hell, a couple of the players actually carried their sticks into the stands." Salen went on, "I also hope that exposing the players to people in other walks of life in these educational programs will make them less likely to do the really stupid things like stealing and brawling and abusing their wives or girlfriends."

"I hope so," said Kress. "Hell, some of my players think that the merchandise in stores is free to them because of their celebrity status. Shit, I had a Miami ball player arrested for walking away from a fruit stand with a grapefruit. When the cop asked him why he didn't pay for it, the arrogant asshole told him, 'hell, I pick 'em off trees all the time. This jest savin' me reachin' up. Ain't no big deal.' But unfortunately the stand owner didn't feel that way. The damn player makes a million bucks a year and he steals a grapefruit. Go figure."

"Well," said Salen, "let's hope this program works. I can't see how it can hurt them."

"No, neither can I," said Kress. "Maybe they'll get involved with music, and we can have a pro player's choir in the future.

Salen added, "Or the pro athlete sewing circle or book club."

"We all agree that we cannot see how this can make things worse or cause them to get into more trouble," replied Kress as they ended their phone call.

Obviously, the commissioners who held that opinion were not aware of the upcoming Sarasota 'Trash Talk' Symposium.

The press release that emanated from the commissioners' meeting was a bombshell to the fans as well as the players. A seminal moment in sports history. No one had ever required professional athletes in the United States to get continuing education other than in their sport. Some of the athletes were not required to have any education, although there had not yet been reports of anyone leaving high school to sign a professional contract before graduation.

There was mixed reaction from the public. Some thought it absurd. They looked at these players as gladiators, as pieces of meat to be put in the arena for the pleasure of the public. Others thought the program was a waste of money and would surely result in an increase in ticket prices. But the majority of the public seemed to think that it was a clever and reasonable approach to improving the image of professional athletes.

The topic occupied radio talk shows for weeks. Imus was laughing so hard at comments from callers he almost choked on a bagel. Mitch Albom in Detroit ran a call-in survey and found seventy percent of the callers favored the new requirement.

Leno and Letterman created an entire repertoire of athlete-education jokes. Letterman suggested a Montessori program might be instituted. A guest on Leno's show suggested a company be formed to make steel piano benches in case any athlete decided to take up that noble instrument.

On ESPN, sports commentators came on screen with piles of textbooks in front of them, and one wore a mortarboard.

Terry Bradshaw and Howie Long said that they would take postgraduate courses since they were retired. Everyone seemed to get their laughs from the plan, but a real curiosity was created about future activities and results.

The athletes, with very few exceptions, were irate. They saw no reason to waste their time, and no need to change anything about themselves. And they certainly could not imagine an educational program that would gain their interest or benefit them in any way. Obviously, they were not yet aware of the upcoming Sarasota 'Trash Talk' symposium.

It was 8:20 A.M. when Jordy walked into Arnie's office. This was the earliest Jordy had arrived at work in months, and he was eager that Arnie know he was there. He practically skipped into the office and was halfway into a cheery, "Good morning Arnie. How the hell —" but he stopped mid-sentence when he saw the distraught look on Arnie's face as he sat at his desk with chin resting on his right fist, elbow bent on the desk. "What the hell happened to you? You look like you fell out of the wrong side of the bed this morning."

"You won't believe this," said Arnie with a deep breath and then a sigh. "I just got a call from the national office. From old Ed Mundhill himself."

"The big boss called you already this morning?" said Jordy, impressed. "Anything really important?"

"Yeah, Jordy, damned important. He wants us to change the meeting theme."

"What?" shouted Jordy. "It's a great theme. Look at all the work we've already done. Everybody's excited about it. We're even getting registrants already. We can't change now. That's a bunch of crap."

"Hey, I agree," replied Arnie. "I told all of that to Mundhill. Not exactly in your words, but I was pretty strong. He said he'll think about it, but he wants us to submit a couple of alternatives."

"Have you told Schriff yet?" Jordy asked.

"No, he's not in yet, but I'll grab him as soon as he gets here. We need some strong support from him if we are going to convince Mundhill to let us keep our theme. I hope that Rama has it in him to stand up for us."

"Me too," replied Jordy, "but I wouldn't bet my life on it."

"Well Jordy, you better start thinking of a few new possibilities for themes. Tell Pam and Melissa too. I'll do everything I can to change Mr. Mundhill's mind."

"Okay, Arnie. Let me know how things are going after you talk with Schriff."

Jordy left the office without even remembering to impress Arnie with his early arrival. It didn't seem very important now.

Arnie was at Rama Schriff's office door at 9:02, two minutes after Mr. Schriff arrived. Schriff was seated at his very neat desk moving a few sheets of paper onto small neat piles.

"Rama," Arnie burst in, "I've got to talk to you about a serious problem. I got —"

He was interrupted by Schriff. "Serious problem?" Schriff's Indian accent was very strong at this moment indicating some distress. "What can be so serious so early in the workday?"

"It's Mundhill," Arnie went on. "He's —"

But once again Schriff interrupted. "Mundhill? You mean Edmund Mundhill? Our president?"

"The one and only," Arnie said sarcastically. "He wants a different meeting theme."

"What?" shouted Schriff in a near screech. "Different theme? It's too late. Didn't he already approve the present one?"

"Well, not exactly," said Arnie. "We never asked him. We just sent the tentative program and the title."

"Never asked him?" Schriff now squeaked. It sounded a bit like a question, but he didn't wait for an answer. He started again. "Oh, my, my, my, Arnie, Arnie, how could you not ask him?"

"I thought it was our call, Rama," Arnie explained.

"Oh my, oh my, Arnie. Our call? We have no call. He is our president. He is my boss. Oh, oh, oh."

"Calm down, Rama," Arnie softened his tone. "I'll figure some way to convince Mundhill that our topic is very important and very appropriate."

"Oh, yes. Yes, yes, Arnie. Please do so," wailed Schriff. "I am now leaving for a massage. I must go now, Arnie. I will return tomorrow morning. Thank you, Arnie. Thank you." With that he slid back his chair and bolted from the office.

Arnie just shook his head slowly back and forth, and walked back toward his office to plan a strategy.

Arnie spent the rest of the day alone in his office with the door closed. He skipped lunch and let all the phone calls Melissa didn't answer go to his message service. He wrote notes on a tablet. Half of the time he scratched them out and rewrote them. Arnie mumbled to himself and ran his hands through his hair as he leaned back in his desk chair.

By six o'clock Arnie knew what he had to do. He sighed, pushed his chair back from the desk, got up, switched off the office light, and left.

When Arnie got to his apartment, he kicked off his shoes, threw a leftover slice of pizza into the microwave, and did something that he only did about three times a year. He opened a can of Miller Lite beer. Arnie tossed the hot slice of pizza onto a paper plate, grabbed a paper napkin and his beer, and flopped on the couch. As he punched on the TV set to the 6:30 world news, he thought, tomorrow is going to be one hell of a day.

Arnie awakened on the couch. It was dark outside, and he was in his work clothes. The living room lamp and the TV were on. He looked at the clock: 1:23 A.M. He arose, stretched, staggered to the bedroom after turning off the TV and lamp, and undressed. He fell onto the bed without even brushing his teeth. He clicked the bedroom lamp off and was asleep again within a minute.

At 3:00 A.M. Arnie awoke. He had been dreaming something about Mr. Mundhill. His heart was racing. He didn't remember the details, but he remembered shooting Mundhill. He jumped up, got a glass of water, and tried to wash away the beer and pizza taste while his heart slowed to normal.

The remainder of the night was spent tossing and turning in bed. Arnie thought that he may have slept thirty or forty minutes when his alarm went off: 6:00 A.M. Work time. Showered, shaved, and dressed and with the fresh taste of toothpaste in his mouth, Arnie hopped into his car and headed for work.

The beautiful Sarasota sunrise made him feel somewhat better, but Arnie was not at his peak when he arrived at his office. Since it was not quite 7:30, no one else was there yet. Arnie made a pot of coffee, stood watching it brew, and then took a cup after the pot beeped to signal the coffee was ready. He went to his office, turned on the light, closed the door, sat in his chair, and stared at the wall while he sipped his coffee. Arnie checked his watch every five minutes. Time was creeping by. 7:55 A.M. It was 6:55 A.M. in Omaha. Arnie knew that it was useless to call before 7:30 Omaha time. Although the word was that Mundhill was usually in by 6:30.

By 7:00 a.m. Omaha time, Arnie could wait no longer and punched in Mundhill's office number.

Mundhill answered on the first ring. "Mundhill here," was his barked greeting.

"Good morning, Mr. Mundhill. This is Arnie Schwartz."

There was a pause.

"From the Sarasota office." A slight upward lilt made it sound like a question.

"Hello, Schwartz. What can I do for you? You have a new theme?" grumbled Mundhill.

"Well, no, sir," said Arnie sounding timid.

"That's what I wanted to tell you about. I've given a lot of thought to our discussion yesterday, and I conferred with the people here at the office and, well, we think trash is an excellent topic."

"Oh, hell," roared Mundhill. "It makes me think of a bad R-rated movie. Damn it, can't you people use a little imagination?"

Arnie broke in, "That's just it, Mr. Mundhill. We've used a lot of imagination. It took hours and hours of discussion for our team to pick the theme and title. We reviewed a hundred or more potential topics. We canvassed several members of the society. That was a bit of an embellishment by Arnie, but his courage was mounting. "And every one agreed that trash talk is a great title and a great theme. We have some fantastic speakers committed. This will be the best meeting in the history of the society."

Arnie thought that the lack of sleep must be affecting his brain. Was he on the road to unemployment? There was a long, quiet interval and Arnie thought he had lost the connection or Mundhill had quietly hung up. "Mr. Mundhill, I guarantee you a great meeting."

"Schwartz, you are a gutsy son of a gun. I'll say that much for you. Is Schriff in agreement with you?"

"He sure is," shouted Arnie with more enthusiasm than normal. "He is thrilled with the topic and the plans so far. I think it made him think of his homeland and their issues and really got him excited," Arnie improvised.

"Well, that's surprising," said Mundhill. After a long pause, he said. "I'll tell you what, Schwartz. I'll let you go ahead. But if this flops or embarrasses us, I guarantee I'll have your balls and Schriff's."

"No problem," cried Arnie with glee.

"Keep me up to date on your progress," said Mundhill and hung up.

As Arnie hung up the phone, happy as he could possibly be and wide awake, a thought went through his mind, does Schriff have any?

He smiled to himself as he left his office to inform the group of his triumph. Schriff would be all right too as long as Arnie omitted the guarantee he made to Mundhill and especially the "guarantee" Mundhill made to him.

Ed Mundhill sat behind his desk at the national office of the Environmentalist Society in Omaha, Nebraska. At fifty-seven-years-old Mundhill was finishing his ninth year as president of the society. He was wondering if he could make it through ten years, which would fulfil his second five-year contract. Sitting, staring out of the window through his wire-rimmed glasses, his hands folded on his flat stomach, his legs extended as he slouched in his desk chair, he muttered, "How long can I do this? The job's all right, but I miss getting out in the field, and Omaha is killing me."

Ed Mundhill grew up in Pittsburgh, Pennsylvania. Actually, in Crafton, a small suburb of Pittsburgh. After college he left his beloved city to pursue a master's degree in environmental science at Purdue University. That's where he met Sally Urquart. They hit it off, and by the end of his second year, he had both a master's degree and a new wife. They made an interesting couple, Ed a solemn and brooding person who was quiet most of the time and Sally, a perky, pleasant, and talkative woman. They moved from West Lafayette, Indiana, to Madison, Wisconsin, where Ed had landed a job with the Forest Service and Sally as a first-grade teacher.

Ed liked the Forest Service where he worked in the field, testing for everything from tree health to water availability to erosion to forest thinning. He was happy. He liked working alone or with people who didn't look for constant discussion. But after three years, the Forest Service moved him, and then they moved him twice more over the next seven years.

Although Sally did not get pregnant during these years, Ed was not disappointed since the frequent moves created a difficult lifestyle and increasing tension in their marriage. Sally began to be less of an extrovert as job opportunities became more difficult and finally disappeared. Ed became even less talkative, to the point of almost mute, and spent more and more time on the job. He became a man of no hobbies, no humor and, after the fourth move, no wife. Sally packed up. When Ed left for Albuquerque, she went to Chicago, and a new teaching job and a new life.

The divorce papers reached Ed shortly after he settled in Albuquerque, and he signed them without argument. He understood Sally's decision, and he realized he liked being alone better. Then, nine years ago, having supervised many field projects, he was courted by the National Environmentalist Society to become their president.

As he stared out his office window, Mundhill thought about his situation. I work with a bunch of jerks, but fortunately I don't really interact with them except by e-mail. And the board members are a bunch of asses who don't understand how little they know. But they're a spineless bunch, and so they back down every time I challenge them.

Well at least I got rid of that bitch of a secretary I inherited when I arrived. I couldn't stand her incessant chatter and her bossiness. Firing her felt good, but the dammed crying almost got to me. Wailing about her twenty years with the organization, you'd have thought she'd run the place. It was a lot easier firing her replacement. That dummy lasted just seven months. What a dodo. Now I've got Betty. Quiet, mousy Betty. If she'd stop flinching when I tell her to do something, it would be okay. But she's no bother, and she's halfway competent.

Mundhill got up and went to the small refrigerator, got a can of Sprite, sat back down at his desk, and looked around. "Well, when you get right down to it, this job's not too bad. No one can tell me what to do, and the local offices shake every time I call them for fear I'll ream their asses about something they're doing wrong."

He was having difficulty believing that trash talk was a worthy topic for a national meeting of his society. He did have to admit that garbage, or trash, as his colleagues preferred to call it, was a serious problem. But he thought if this meeting gets screwed up at all, I'll have all the reason I need to dump that wishy-washy Schriff and that pain in the ass Schwartz. That thought brought a rare smile to his face.

In the history of professional sports in the United States, there had never before been a meeting of the boards of the players unions from the NBA, NFL, NHL, and MLB. This dictum from the commissioners of each of those sports, that all players must undergo continuing education in areas other than their sport, rocked the world of these professional athletes.

Sterling Parsch, the president of the NFL Players Association, ranted, "What the fuck do they think we are? Doctors or something? Shit, we ain't stickin' our fingers up people's asses to find out if they're sick and we ain't lookin' into their brains. Why the shit should we have to go listen to lectures and read books and things. All the culture I want, I get in the bars with those sweet, big-boobed babes dancin' in every city we play. They're teachin' me everything I want to know."

"Hey," said Bill Gladley, the player representative from the NBA, "maybe learning a little more about art and music and politics will help us. I don't think it's so bad."

"That's 'cause you went to Princeton," chimed in Rex Hall, the hockey players' rep, "so you think all that stuff's great. Christ, I went to Southern Saskatoon Middle School. I'll have to go looking for spelling bees."

It was clear that there was little happiness in the halls and fields of professional sports. It was March — the off-season for many of the athletes. And the commissioners wanted the cultural, educational activities to start now.

Bobby Bends, the star of the Portland Giants, and one of the greatest home run hitters of all time, jumped into the discussion. "Hey guys, I saw an interesting ad in the newspaper a couple days ago that may provide at least one opportunity. It was about a meeting in Sarasota, Florida, in May that really sounds fascinating. We baseball players won't be able to go since it's during our season, but you other guys can. And in fact, it's more suited to you lowlives anyway," he said with a big grin.

Bobby reached into his shirt pocket and pulled out a paper that he unfolded. "This was in the *Portland Tribune* two days ago, and I tore it out to bring to this meeting. Look at this. Some group called SES is havin' a meeting in Sarasota on trash talk. That's right in line with your specialty in basketball and football and even you hockey guys, although you're more into trashin' than talkin'."

"Lemme see that," said Parsch as he tore it from Bends's hand. "Holy shit, don't that take the cake. Man, this is an answer to our prayers. We can satisfy those jack-off commissioners while we polish up our skills. Hey, it says here we can learn from the experts. Shit, nobody contacted me, and I am the fuckin' Mick Jagger of trash talk. I am the star trash talker of professional sports."

Parsch's statement was met with whistles and boos from his colleagues as they all left their seats to get a look at the ad.

The news of a four-day meeting on trash talk spread through the informal network of pro athletes faster than any newspaper could carry it. And it created more chatter among the players than anything since the previous NFL Commissioner was caught in a hotel room in New Orleans, dressed in panties and a bra and being thrown around by three professional lady wrestlers dressed only in football shoulder pads and helmets.

Jordy couldn't believe the success of his ad campaign, and Arnie couldn't believe what was happening. It was mid-April, and they now had almost 500 registrants. In the first two weeks of April, they got more than double the number of registrants than in all the time prior to that. Arnie had to spend two days negotiating another thirty rooms at the Hyatt. But 130 rooms — even with two persons per room — left him far short of what was needed. Most of the more recent applicants were requesting single rooms with king-size beds. These late registrants didn't even mind when they were told that there were not enough programs printed, and so they would not receive their information packages until they arrived in Sarasota. Jordy's ads were sure drawing some newcomers to the environmentalists meeting.

Arnie was schizophrenic. He was thrilled with the incredible degree of interest in environmental issues, but was panicked regarding the logistics. He was also very puzzled about the interest in single rooms regardless of price. That's what the office help had been told by many of the registrants who had phoned recently. The office staff assumed that their environmental groups must be more affluent than those with which they were familiar. Arnie and Mr. Schriff had never even heard of the Orioles or Cardinals or Hornets and some of these other environmental groups. So they had instructed the office staff, and in particular the temporary help that they had employed to handle the extra work and phone calls, to not even ask for affiliations any longer.

Arnie had received two calls from Ed Mundhill since he'd gotten the go-ahead for the theme. Mundhill expressed some amazement at the attendance figures and questioned who these attendees were. At each call he reminded Arnie of the dire consequences of a screw-up. What did Arnie tell Mr. Schriff? He told his boss that his boss's boss was happy with the progress.

With help from Pamela, Arnie and Melissa scoured the area for more accommodations. Reluctantly Arnie had reserved forty single rooms in the new Ritz-Carlton. But the late registrants had gobbled them up with no concern about rates. This shocked and relieved Arnie. He was able to get another fifteen rooms at the Ritz, which also were immediately claimed by another horde of registrants.

Arnie and his staff worked diligently to cover all bases. More rooms were reserved at the Holiday Inn on Route 41 and a few other motels until finally they believed they had enough. They booked a large block of tickets at the Van Wezel for the Kenny Rogers show on Tuesday, the 28th of May. The ballroom at the Hyatt, now expanded to its maximum size, was booked for an opening-night mixer on Sunday and a major banquet on Wednesday. Arnie wished now that the registration fee was higher than the $100 charged, but that had been a major issue at the last national meeting when many of the attendees complained about the increase from $75 to $100. Fortunately, the Van Wezel tickets had to be paid for separately by those attending the performance. This year there was little complaint about the $100 registration and, in fact, some of the late registrants had asked on the phone whether that was a daily fee.

It was all sort of puzzling to Arnie and the rest of the committee, but as the arrangements began to fall in place, they were overcome with a feeling of joy and excitement. Arnie was so pleased that he was taking the committee to the Bijou Café, one of Sarasota's more upscale restaurants, for an end-of-the-week dinner this Friday evening. He was even more pleased that he was able to convince Mr. Schriff that this was a business expense.

The dinner was a festive event. Arnie, the first to order, chose shrimp cocktail and filet mignon and a Caesar salad in order to show the lack of limits and encourage the others to order anything they wanted regardless of price. Melissa, trying to watch her diet, had a mixed salad with vinaigrette dressing for a starter and blackened grouper, her favorite seafood. Pam, less inhibited and less worried about her plumpness, ordered a crab cake appetizer and veal Milanese. She loved the breaded, pounded veal chop and not many restaurants served it. All the while she was ordering she was thinking of the desserts.

"Does the chocolate soufflé have to be ordered in advance?" she asked the waiter, and was assured that it could be quickly prepared if ordered at the end of dinner.

Jordy threw caution to the wind and reverted

back to his affluent teen years when his parents took him to dinner often and at the very best upscale San Diego restaurants. "I believe I'll try the foie gras appetizer, a Caesar salad, and the breast of duck with raspberry sauce. Hopefully I'll still have room for that soufflé."

The waiter beamed as he took the order.

Finally Arnie ordered a modestly priced bottle of champagne.

And before starting on their appetizers, they toasted each other and had a special toast to Jordy for the most successful ad campaign in the history of the National Environmentalist Society. At least as far as they knew. They ran through the arrangements during dinner. Media rooms secured, enough hotel rooms — hopefully — meals arranged for some days and restaurant lists to be provided for others. Taxi companies and the Tampa and Sarasota airports were notified. A shuttle was arranged from the Sarasota airport to the hotels on Sunday and Monday and back to the airport on Thursday and Friday. Lists of activities in the area were printed up as part of the meeting package. Inexpensive briefcases made of a biodegradable material were ordered and received. Tablets of recycled paper and a pen, also biodegradable, were placed in the briefcases along with the meeting agenda and all of the helpful lists. All speakers were confirmed, audiovisual needs determined, and equipment secured.

With three weeks to go, the committee was pleased that arrangements were in place. Dinner was good, the wine was pleasant, and the ambience of the Bijou Café was comforting. Life was good for Arnie and his committee.

It was Saturday, May 25 at about 5:00 P.M. when Chuck Barkey and Max Gordon deplaned at the Sarasota Airport. Max was happy to be traveling with Chuck, who had not only been a great player before he retired and became a TV sports announcer, but was up there with the best of the trash talkers. Max was hoping to optimize what he could learn at the meeting by hanging around with Chuck. In addition, Chuck had a reputation for finding fun spots and attracting women wherever he went. Some even referred to him as the most eligible bachelor in the country. Max was hopeful. Since they had come a day early, the shuttle was not available so they cabbed it to the Ritz-Carlton, which was only about ten minutes away.

"Not a bad lookin' place," said Chuck, "but looks a little dull. Hey cabby, any hot spots in town?"

"Yeah," said Max, "where the hot chicks hang out."

"Ain't too much around, boys," said the cab driver, a thin, wrinkled, black man with white hair who looked about eighty years old. "But they's a few. One over at the quay close to your hotel, then there's the Outer Limit and a couple others. You can start there."

"Thanks pal," said Barkey as they pulled up in the driveway of the Ritz-Carlton. He handed the driver a $20 bill for the $6 ride and said, "Keep the change. Thanks for the info."

"Thank you, sir. That's mighty generous. Enjoy your stay." And away he went to look for another fare.

"Man, this looks pretty nice. Not bad digs for a little city," said Max.

"Yessiree, Max," said Barkey as they entered the lobby trailed by the bellman carrying their two suitcases. Barkey spotted the very attractive young lady behind the registration counter.

"Hello, ma'am," said Chuck. "We'd like to check in."

She looked up and her eyes widened in a look of surprise. "Why certainly. Hey, you're Chuck Barkey, the basketball guy, aren't you? I've seen you on TV."

"That's me, honey," said Barkey, "and I'm here in Sarasota just for you."

"Sure," said Leona, which was the name on her badge, that also said "trainee."

"I see you're a trainee and, luckily, I'm a 'trainer,' " said Chuck.

"Yes, I bet you say that to all female trainees. Why are you here in Sarasota?"

"We're here for the Trash Talk meeting," said Max.

"That's right," said Chuck. "Meet my friend Max Gordon. He plays for Orlando."

"I'm surprised you guys have so much interest in the environment," said Leona.

Max and Chuck, puzzled, just looked at each other.

Chuck responded, "We love this environment. The Ritz-Carlton is our favorite hotel and you make this environment heavenly."

"Oh brother," Leona responded. "I better get you checked in before I faint from the compliments."

Leona was a striking beauty at five feet eight and one hundred fifteen pounds with long shining auburn hair and almond eyes. Although only twenty-five-years-old, she could hold her own with anyone. She was an army brat, born of a Filipino mother and an American father who was a career officer in the military. Her father had met and married Leona's mother while he was stationed in Manila, and Leona was born one year later. The family was transfered numerous times, so Leona went to elementary school in Georgia, high school in California, college at Bryn Mawr outside of Philadelphia, and got an MBA at Columbia University in Manhattan. The last was not chosen because of family location but rather because of the reputation of the Columbia business program and Leona's desire to live in "the big city." Throughout her academic years, Leona was an outstanding student. She was the valedictorian of both her high school and college graduating classes. She was also an outstanding tennis player at both the high school and college levels and an all-conference basketball player in high school. Her varied life experiences and outstanding personality gave her a maturity well beyond her years. In a word, Leona was dynamite, and even a Chuck Barkey did not intimidate her.

"Hey Max," said Chuck as they got on the elevator to go to their rooms, "let's get together at about seven-thirty here in the lobby and check out the town and get some dinner."

"Sounds good, Chuck. Catch you at seven-thirty, no ties just sport shirts. Okay?"

The big day finally arrived. As Arnie drove north on route 41 from his two-room apartment near Phillipe Creek, it took all the control he had not to greatly exceed the speed limit. He had gotten one speeding ticket in his driving life and that had been right here on Route 41 and for only six miles over the 45-mile-per-hour limit. Ever since that incident seven years ago, Arnie had remained a law abiding citizen. Today, however, he felt like throwing caution to the wind and so held his nine-year-old Toyota right at fifty with a new feeling of power and authority. This week Sarasota was his city!

Arnie drove first to Sarasota airport where he

was relieved to see signs outside the baggage claim area indicating a shuttle stop for attendees of the Trash Talk Conference. He stopped the car and hopped out quickly to take a look around and make sure there were some signs inside. As he got a quick look inside the door and noted at least one sign, an airport policeman blew his whistle and told Arnie to get his car out of there or it'd be towed.

If he only knew who I was, Arnie thought. He had been disappointed that an article in the *Sarasota Herald Tribune* about the conference didn't have his picture. He mentioned that to Jordy and hoped that during the conference a newspaper picture of him might run.

Arnie arrived at the Hyatt at 10:13 A.M. Melissa and Pam were there in the registration area of the convention center. Trash Talk signs with Jordy's garbage can picture were on easels in several areas of the hotel and the attached convention center lobby.

Arnie spotted Jordy across the way talking with a photographer and went over to say hello.

"Well Arnie, things look great" said Jordy. "This is Gary Fraise, our photographer. Gary, this is Arnie Schwartz, head of the conference committee."

They shook hands, and Gary assured Arnie

that he would capture the action during the conference.

Pam and Melissa ushered Arnie around to look in all the meeting rooms as well as the grand ballroom. Everything appeared to be in good shape. The meeting rooms looked well equipped with audiovisual equipment, water pitchers, paper cups that were environmentally friendly and flip charts with lovely yellowish tan recycled paper pads. The ballroom was set-up with tables for eight people, and large, banquet-type tables in the center of the room and a few other locations, where hors d'oeuvres would be set out at 6:00 P.M. Two bars, as yet unstocked, were set up, one at each end of the ballroom. "Trash Talk" posters on easels were evident near the wall in several places around the room and a large WELCOME CONFEREES sign hung at the end farthest from the main doors.

Arnie went with Pam and Melissa to check the registration desk. Jordy left the photographer and joined them. There were three young women hired as temporary employees to handle the registration. Pam and Melissa intended to help out.

"Well guys, 518 registrants. Can you believe it?" Jordy crowed.

"It's incredible," said Pam. "I talked with some folks from the national office and they have never had more than about 200 — I think 205. They can't get over it. I told them they can thank Jordy's ads and the beauty of Sarasota. And I also told them that a whole lot of people appreciate Florida's environmentalist mentality and that helped attract a bigger group as well."

"Hey, whatever," said Arnie, "let's just keep our fingers crossed that all goes smoothly. By the way, have any of you seen Ed Mundhill? I'm not really looking forward to running into him, but he certainly should be happy with everything here."

None of the others had seen him. Melissa commented, "I understand that nothing ever makes him happy, but at least he shouldn't be angry with us."

They all laughed.

"Let's split up the list of speakers, and we'll each start to check and see if they've arrived yet and if they have any special needs for their presentations," Arnie suggested. "I expect that in a couple of hours this place is going to be a madhouse."

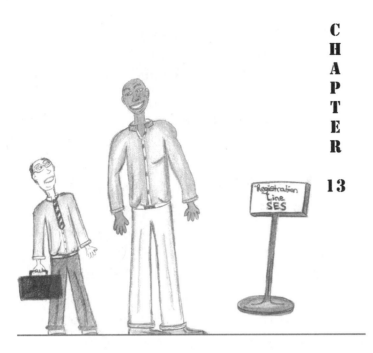

Pam and Melissa looked concerned as they rushed into Arnie's makeshift office in a small conference room at the edge of the convention center.

Arnie had secluded himself in the office at about one o'clock and closed the door so he could concentrate on reviewing the program one more time.

"Arnie, you've got to come out here and take a look at the registration line," said Melissa breathlessly.

"It's weird," added Pam. "You gotta take a look."

"Hey guys, I'm busy. I'll take a look in about fifteen minutes."

"No," urged Pam. "Come and look now. Please."

Arnie reluctantly pushed himself away from the desk and out of his chair grumbling about interruptions and began to follow. "What's so interesting about a registration line?" he asked as they went through the doorway. But as he moved into the registration center, he froze and his mouth dropped open.

"What the hell?" He couldn't believe his eyes. The line was long and that was good. But what was so strange is that it looked like a very uneven picket fence. Very uneven! There were the average-looking environmentalists, many of whom Arnie knew — or they looked familiar from past meetings. But they were outnumbered by groups of what looked to Arnie like giants interspersed in the registration line, some alone but most in groups of anywhere from two to six or seven.

They were all men, far more black men than white, and they were bigger than anyone that Arnie had ever seen. Some were tall big and a little on the thin side. But many were big-big — tall and heavy. Arnie thought that many must be almost seven feet and a large number were probably more than three hundred pounds! Who were they and where did they come from? Arnie wondered. Were these guys that were involved in operating equipment like compactors? He had never seen them at any other environmentalist society meetings. This trash topic must have excited a whole new group that never attended the past meetings.

He was about to suggest to Pam and Melissa that they go and talk to a few of them and maybe to some of the regulars as well, since many of the usual-sized environmentalists kept gawking up at these others as though they were trying to see a woodpecker in a giant redwood tree. The large guys also seemed to know one another, and they were a lot louder than the average society member.

But before Arnie got the words out, Jordy came rushing up. As he began pushing Arnie, Pam, and Melissa back toward Arnie's office, he said in a breathless, panicky voice. "Oh man, have we got some problems."

"Whatdaya mean?" said Arnie.

"Are those people anti-environmental protestors?" asked Pam.

"No, no," cried Jordy. "Shit. You won't believe what's happened. My ad! That great ad! Holy shit. It said come to the Trash Talk Conference. Well, I just talked to two of those guys and do you know who they are?"

Three simultaneous "nos" accompanied by

vigorous back and forth shaking of the three heads was the identical response from Pam, Melissa, and Arnie.

"Well," continued Jordy, "the two I talked to are professional basketball players and —"

But before he could continue Melissa cried out, "Oh god, they came to the wrong meeting."

"No," shouted Jordy. "*They* think they're at the right meeting. Trash Talk to them means insulting each other by swearing and saying bad things and insulting people on the other team so they get upset and angry and it screws up their game. They told me that almost all the pros in all the sports do it. And they said it's really an art and it's really cool and when they saw the ad they jumped on this meeting. Hell, they're here to brush up their skills. They think that we have experts. Wait till they see the program. We'll be dead! Oh, Jesus Christ, what are we gonna do now? This could be the biggest disaster in the history of the Environmentalist Society. Hell, it could be the biggest disaster in the history of Sarasota! Hell, the country!"

They were cooked!

Arnie thought of Mundhill and unconsciously reached down to his crotch.

Chuck Barkey and Max Gordon were the first of the athletes to actually get registered and receive their registration materials in the neat yellowish-brown biodegradable cloth-like briefcase. They were earlier than most of their colleagues since they had arrived in Sarasota the day before to scope out the city night life. That had not gone all that well. They had wandered out of the hotel and walked a few blocks where they found a nice restaurant called Monroes. Their waiter had informed them that Monroes had a "night club" upstairs and they might just want to drop in up there after dinner. It sounded good. Dinner was fine, although Max could have eaten three of the steaks rather than just the one delicate cut that he had received. Chuck liked the ahi tuna as well as the shrimp cocktail appetizer. He was a bit more used to dining out in the elite style than was Max, who generally found an "all-you-can-eat" buffet restaurant when he was traveling with the team.

"When you're six feet eleven and about three hundred pounds, you ain't lookin for the nine ounce cut," he told Chuck.

Chuck got a kick out of Max, although at six foot six and two-hundred-forty pounds, Chuck could have handled another filet or two of that ahi.

"Well," said Chuck, "maybe some peanuts and pretzels with the beer upstairs will carry us over until you get to bite into some pretty young thing's thigh."

"Hey, that's for me," said Max. They paid their bill and went upstairs to the club. Most of the other patrons were well beyond fifty, although they did manage to sit next to a couple of attractive young ladies at the end of the bar.

"Well, hello," said Chuck. "Hope you're here for the Trash Talk conference."

"The what?" said one of the two.

"Trash Talk conference?" said the second.

"No, we're just here on layover until tomorrow. We're Delta Airline attendants and we just flew in from St. Louis today."

"Well," said Max, "We would like to lay over with you!"

"Oh sure," said the blond with a giggle. "And we can talk trash all night!"

"No shi — I mean no kidding," said Max. "Wouldn't you like to do something exciting with us two debonair gentlemen?"

The two looked at each other. This wasn't their first encounter with the likes of these two.

"Hey, I'll tell you what," said the cute redhead. "Let's take the romantic Gulf cruise. It leaves from just a couple blocks from here and we can have drinks and music and who knows what."

"Sounds great," said Max enthusiastically.

He and Chuck both missed the wink between the redhead and blond.

The "romantic gulf cruise" turned out to be a two-and-a-half-hour boat ride on a barge with palm trees in buckets of dirt placed around the perimeter of the boat. The music was primarily Hawaiian luau in nature and the drinks consisted of fruit punch with or without rum. With rum the drinks were two dollars. Without rum, the juice drinks were included in the twenty-dollar ticket for the cruise. Three hours later and with terrible rum headaches, Chuck and Max were headed back to the Ritz alone. Brenda and Joan said that they had a great evening, learned a lot about posting up and fast breaks, as well as gaining some insight into the psychology of trash talk. But, since they were required to have at least eight hour's sleep before working a flight, and they had to be at the airport at 10 A.M., they were calling it a night.

"Welcome to Sarasota," said Chuck as he got off the elevator on his floor, two below Max. "I'll meet you for brunch at eleven tomorrow, and then we'll go register for the meeting.

"Good night," said Max. "Sweet dreams."

Max and Chuck carried their registration packages over to the Boat House, which was the restaurant and bar attached to the Hyatt.

"Come on, Chuck. I'll buy you a beer and we can look at this stuff," said Max.

"I'll settle for coffee," retorted Chuck. "I'm still rum soaked."

They sat at one of the small, wooden tables in the bar area and, after giving the waitress their order, they opened their briefcases and pulled out a stack of papers. Chuck was the first to open the pamphlet marked PROGRAM, and then the shit hit the fan!

"What the fuck?" said Max.

Chuck's only response was, "Holy shit."

"What is this, Chuck? We musta signed in at the wrong place."

"Can't be," said Chuck. "This ugly bag they gave us says TRASH TALK CONFERENCE."

"Holy shit."

Both stood in unison and grabbed their stuff.

"Fuck the beer," said Max.

Chuck didn't answer and they both hurried back toward the registration area.

As they reentered the registration area they just about ran into Bernie "Too Fat" McCann. Mc-Cann was the six foot five, four hundred six pound offensive tackle from Green Bay. In his youth Bernie had revered the former defensive end from Dallas, Ed "Too Tall" Jones. When Bernie was a teenager, he was tall for his age and kept referring to himself as "Too Tall McCann." But, as he gained more and more weight, his buddies changed that to "Too Fat McCann," and that name had followed him through the University of Miami and on to Green Bay. Too Fat McCann was also touted to have the biggest butt in the history of the NFL. Although not official, it was claimed to be sixty-three inches wide.

Too Fat was in the process of bitching to a friend of his, Randy Wilson. Wilson, not small himself at six feet seven and two hundred forty-five pounds, was a forward with the Atlanta basketball team. Evidently Too Fat had also arrived in Sarasota on Saturday and, while exploring the town, walked over to the marina where he watched people parasailing, that is, being pulled by a speedboat while harnessed to a parachute attached to the boat by a long rope. Too Fat had been fascinated. It looked like great fun to sail along that high up in the air and get such a great view of the shoreline. He'd decided to give it a try. The three parasail employees paled when they saw Too Fat approaching.

"Hey, I'd like to give that a try," said Too Fat.

The three men looked at each other and had a very animated conversation in Spanish.

After a minute or two, one turned to Too Fat and said, "Sir, I'm not sure we can take you."

Before he could say more, Too Fat said, "What the hell you talkin' about," and he pulled out two one hundred dollar bills and handed them to the man. "Sign says 'Parasail Here' and I'm a payin' customer."

More discussion in Spanish followed and, with the realization that this guy was willing to pay two hundred dollars for a forty-dollar ride, they said okay.

They had to fasten three harnesses together,

but they finally fitted Too Fat in the harnesses and hooked him to the parachute. With Too Fat in the harness standing in the appropriate spot on the boat platform, ready to lift off once the boat reached adequate speed to fill the parachute with air, the boat took off. One of the three crew members stood near Too Fat, one was lookout for any other boats or swimmers, and one drove. As the boat reached it's maximum speed of about thirty miles an hour, the parachute filled with air, but Too Fat never budged. The boat screamed along with the frustrated crew praying for wind gusts, but it was hopeless. This load was far too heavy.

Greater speed was needed. They returned to the dock with Too Fat refusing to give up or move. He had paid his money and he wanted to float high in the sky. The three crewman decided to add a second motor from one of the other boats — this one eighty horsepower. After the addition, they headed back into the gulf and up along the shore of Longboat Key. Too Fat had visions of soaring sixty to seventy feet in the air, just like the parasailers he had watched, and getting a really great view of the scenery.

Both engines screamed as the boat achieved it's top speed of about 48 miles per hour, and the driver turned it into the wind to fill the parachute and launch Too Fat into flight.

An eighty-two-year-old man standing on the beach on Longboat Key would later describe to his friends and family what he saw as something he had never seen in thirty-five years of watching parasailers run up and down the shore of Longboat Key. Too Fat and his parachute took the maximum gust of wind and did a para-skip. He lifted off the boat and rose about three feet into the air, but as the boat hit a wave and slowed by about two miles an hour, Too Fat hit the water with that broad ass of his and skittered along the surface for about thirty feet and then, as the boat picked up it's lost speed he lifted again, no more than seven or eight feet before an oncoming wave once again slightly slowed the boat, and Too Fat hit the water again. The octagenarian on shore would tell everyone he spoke with afterward that the big hulk hooked to a parachute and skipping or bouncing along the surface of the water was hightailing it back toward the pier at Marina Jack's when he lost sight of the party.

"It was some sight," he bragged. "Thirty-five years never seen nothin' like that."

Too Fat was dragged back to shore coughing and sputtering and the three crew members and two dock workers pulled him on shore and out of his harness.

As Too Fat staggered away, he swore to himself

that he was staying on solid ground from then on and never getting in a lake or the ocean again. "Shit, football is a hell of a lot safer," he was mumbling as he shakily made his way back to the hotel.

And so, with numerous bruises and still hearing water sloshing inside his ears, Too Fat McCann was at the end of the registration line anxious to get into something a hellava lot better than parasailing. Too Fat loved trash talk.

Barkey and Gordon saw Wilson and McCann at the end of the line and went over to see what they knew about this meeting.

After a quick exchange of greetings and high fives all around, Chuck asked, "Have you guys seen the program for this meeting?"

"No," said Wilson, and McCann shook his head no. "We just got in this registration line."

"Well," said Max, "you're in for a big surprise."

"Oh yeah," said McCann. "What kind, good or bad?"

"Hey," said Chuck Barkey, "I think we have a king-size misunderstanding. Look at these sessions." He pointed to his program. "Biodegradability," "Environmental Impact," and "Disposal Issues Related to the Red Tide," "Where do we go with Dump Sites," and on and on. Does that sound like trash talk to you?"

"It sounds like tree-hugger talk," said Wilson.

"Sounds like some kind of environmental jazz," said McCann.

"Yeah, that's the same conclusion we came up with," piped in Max Gordon. "We got ourselves signed into some fuckin' environmental shit meeting. I think we been screwed."

"How the fuck can that happen?" said McCann.

"I think we've been duped by someone sponsoring this meeting," said Barkey. "Max and I were just on our way to find the bastards who are runnin' this and find out what's goin' on."

"We'll come along," said Wilson. He and Too Fat left the registration line, and the group headed for the door marked OFFICE across the room.

Arnie, Pam, Melissa, and Jordy were hunkered down in the office trying to come to grips with what happened. To make matters even more complicated, Mr. Schriff, the head of the Sarasota Environmentalist's office and their boss, arrived to see how things were going, and was now cloistered in the office with them.

"I am thinking that something is going wrong here," said Mr Schriff. "There is much shouting out there from those large people."

"See, Jordy, that's what comes from false advertising," admonished Arnie, ignoring Mr. Schriff's comments.

"False advertising!" cried Jordy. "You loved my ad."

"Come on, guys," Pam broke in. "Forget the finger pointing. We're all in deep trouble here so let's figure out what we can do."

"Yes," said Melissa, "let's think."

The loud bang on the door almost scared them out of their chairs.

"What the —?" cried Arnie, but before he got any farther the door flew open, and four of the giants charged in. The last one was so wide he came through the door sideways. Arnie and his colleagues reflexively jumped up from their chairs and backed toward a corner of the room.

"What the hell is going on here?" shouted Barkey. "This is no trash talk meeting!"

"It certainly is," Arnie squeaked as he backed into Jordy and Pam in their continued slow retreat toward the corner.

Melissa, looking up at the large intruders from her position behind Jordy and Pam, said, "This is a very important meeting. Trash is a major problem in this country. We need to do something."

Too Fat's eyes widened. "You mean trash — like fuckin' garbage?"

"Yes, of course, garbage and other refuse," said Melissa.

At this point, Mr. Schriff, eyes wide with excitement or maybe fear, announced with a more pronounced Indian accent than usual, "Well, I am believing that things are under control here, and so I will be taking my leave. All is in good hands. Good luck. I will be back for the opening session tomorrow. I must go now to attend to other very important matters —"

And he was gone before anyone could comment.

"Shit," said Wilson. "You mean you conned us into coming all the way to Sarasota to hear about garbage?"

"We did not con you," shouted Jordy. "Our ads and information were perfectly clear. We can't help it if you couldn't understand that this is an environmental meeting."

"Couldn't understand!" shouted Barkey, glaring at Jordy and taking a step forward that caused Jordy to jump back and forced Melissa up against the wall behind them.

Melissa tried to push Jordy off her feet, but he was frozen there.

"Why you little asshole," bellowed Barkey. "You'll understand what I got from your ad when I put my fist in your mouth."

"Wait, wait!" cried Pam, who had faced tense situations on occasion when some of her protest groups were challenged. "Stop screaming and calm down, and we'll figure out a way to accommodate you."

"How the hell you gonna do that?" asked McCann.

"We could give you your money back," Melissa croaked as she was being squashed against the wall by Jordy who seemed to be trying to back through the wall and disappear.

"Hell, that's no help," said Wilson. "We're here and we need credit for the league requirement. We're not backing out of this meeting," he said adamantly.

"That's right," said Gordon. "We want this meeting to satisfy our shit requirement. We ain't gonna leave without attending."

"Well, I agree," said Barkey. "But we're not sittin' through all these bullshit sessions either. You better change your program and get some real trash talkin' sessions in here."

Arnie finally regained some composure, although he was still deathly pale. "Look guys, let's all sit down and talk about this. If you really want to stay for the meeting, and you think your buddies out there will stay, let's see if we can adjust the program."

"Yeah," said Wilson. "Let's adjust the program."

"Okay," said Arnie with a sigh. "Let's act as an ad hoc committee and go through the agenda."

"What the fuck kinda committee?" questioned Too Fat. "Ad what?"

"Just a temporary committee," Arnie responded. "There are four of you and four of us. Let's sit at the table and see what we can do to make you happy."

"Okay," said Barkey. "Sounds reasonable."

They all gathered around the table in Arnie's office as Melissa gave each person a copy of the program and a pen.

Four hours later a sweat-soaked Arnie, a pallid Jordy and Pam and Melissa finally sat back in their chairs feeling somewhere between exhaustion, relief, despair, and panic, but at least satisfied that they had reached a compromise on the days that lay ahead. The four athletes looked fairly satisfied but still on the edge of violence.

The sounds outside the office had gotten louder with occasional shouts and obscenities as more and more athletes realized that what they had signed up for was not what they expected. Several times during the meeting of the ad hoc committee, there were frantic knocks on the door and pleadings by the three temporary employees handling the actual registrations for Arnie to come out and make some kind of announcement to calm down the crowd. Many of the environmentalists in the line were pleading ignorance regarding the situation as they were being threatened by some of the athletes. Four of the hotel security guards, hearing the commotion, had come into the conference lobby, but seeing the size of the athletes and their state of unhappiness, busied themselves by collecting autographs from the enraged complainants.

After the third interruption by a temporary employee, Chuck Barkey jumped up, grabbed Arnie by the upper arm, and said, "C'mon, you and I will go out there and tell them we're working on fixing things."

They went out into the conference lobby and both started shouting.

Arnie was hollering, "Attention, attention," but was totally drowned out.

Barkey, in a booming, baritone voice shouted, "Listen up, listen up. Hey! Listen up."

The crowd quieted, and turned toward the two.

Barkey spoke. "It seems the meeting organizers screwed something up. We're working on the program and will fill you all in soon. Be patient. Cool it. Give us another hour or two. Go have a drink or a hot dog. Take a walk. Come back in an hour."

With that, and amid a buzz of grumbling and questioning, Chuck pushed Arnie back toward the door and into the office and closed the door behind them. But before they could say a word, there was a loud bang-bang on the door. It opened quickly as a rabid looking Edmund Mundhill stormed in. He aimed his dagger stare at Arnie, not even noticing who else was there, and bellowed, "What the hell is going on here? Schwartz, you'd better have one goddamned great explanation for that zoo out there or your job tomorrow will be counting penguins in Antarctica."

Arnie began to stammer, "Mr. Mundhill, we've had a . . . there's been a slight misunderstanding."

"It's a misunderstanding, all right," Mundhill shouted. "I misunderstood your competency. I want an explanation."

A low voice from behind Mundhill said, "Who the fuck are you?" It was Too Fat McCan.

Mundhill swung around and began to reply, "I'll tell you who I am," but he realized he was looking at someone's huge chest. He peered up into the face of the four hundred six-pound football player. Shocked for a moment by McCann's size and menacing stare, Mundhill paused.

Arnie intervened. "Mr. Mundhill is the president of our national society. He is our boss. He's the top person in this whole organization."

Too Fat responded, "Well, Mr. President, we do have a bit of a fuck-up here. Your boys here had us thinkin' this was a real 'trash talk' meetin'. But we come to find its just a 'garbage meetin'. So we and your employees here," Too Fat waved his hand toward Arnie and his team, "are gonna fix it. So don't get your balls in a sling. We'll take care of it. You just get your loud ass out of here so we can get to work."

Mundhill opened his mouth to speak, but no words came out. He turned and pointed at Arnie. He was glaring and hyperventilating. He was so red he looked like he might have a stroke. "Schwartz, I'm going to my room. I will see you tomorrow morning. You and your colleagues, Schriff as well, are about ninety-nine percent of the way out of this society. You are hanging by a thread. Fix this quick or you're all done. I don't know or want to know how this fuck-up occurred, but it better be fixed by tomorrow morning when the sessions start." Mundhill turned and stomped from the room, slamming the door behind him.

In his hotel room Ed Mundhill was a jumble of mixed emotions. He was as angry as a stepped-on snake about the screw-up downstairs. But at the same time he experienced a macabre joy in the suffering he would bring down on that little shit, Schwartz, and that spineless jackass, Rama Schriff.

Why had he ever hired Schriff? Hell, there were twenty society members that he knew that could do the job better. And they were Americans. Why in the hell did the Sarasota board want to hire an Indian to head up a chapter of an American society? He'd been too busy back then to pay attention to such a small office. But now he savored the pleasure of revenge. Never again would he let the board or any of the seventy-three chapters tell him what to do. That thought soothed Mundhill somewhat.

The group of eight finally emerged from Arnie's temporary office and entered the conference lobby. Arnie had called the hotel logistics manager and had her deliver a portable microphone system to him and now stood with the microphone with seven concerned-looking people behind him.

"Your attention please," Arnie shouted into the microphone. "May I please have your attention." With the microphone turned to maximum, Arnie's voice, although shaky, echoed throughout the large lobby. Everyone, environmentalists, athletes, employees, and security guards, as well as some stray hotel guests who were fascinated by this strange gathering, began to look around to see who was speaking.

Maxwell Gordon walked over and grabbed Arnie by the waist and lifted him high into the air. Too Fat pointed at Arnie, who almost dropped his microphone, but managed to speak while Gordon held him about four feet off the ground — until Jordy pushed a chair toward them and Max placed Arnie on it.

"Ladies and Gentlemen. I'm sure that by now you have all realized that there is something strangely different about our environmentalist meeting."

Before he could go any farther, there began a great rumbling and shouts from the athletes.

"What the hell do you mean 'environmentalist meeting'?" yelled one.

"We came for trash talk," hollered another.

"Wait, wait, "shouted Arnie. And he was supported by Barkey and Wilson shouting — without the aid of microphone — for everyone to calm down and listen up. Arnie continued, "There has been a very unfortunate misunderstanding."

The crowd quieted significantly.

"This is the annual meeting of the National Environmentalist Society."

Again a rise of unhappy sounds, but Arnie continued and the moans, groans, and griping died down. "The title, which we, that is the planning committee from the Sarasota chapter came up with — Trash Talk — was meant to be a catchy title to attract environmentalists to come to this meeting to discuss the environmental issues related to trash. What it's doing to the environment, how we can haul it, dispose of it, the various types of trash, hazardous waste, and so forth."

A loud, "Oh shit," was heard from a very large person in the crowd.

"Holy fuck," came out of a stunned looking six foot five, two hundred eighty pounder standing in the front row of the crowd facing Arnie.

Arnie flinched but continued. "We now realize that the title was misleading because to athletes trash talk denotes the activity of verbally insulting each other to affect the opponent's performance."

"You bet your ass that's what it means," shouted an athlete.

"Please," pleaded Arnie. "Let me finish."

There was modest rumbling, but Arnie was able to proceed. "We realized our problem only when all of you arrived here at registration."

"What are ya gonna do about it?" came a shout from the crowd.

"Hang on," yelled Barkey.

Arnie picked up again. "We," and Arnie pointed to the group standing behind him, "spent the last three hours redoing the program to satisfy everyone. Thanks to Mr. Barkey, Mr. Gordon, Mr. Wilson and Mr. Too Fat, I think that we have a modified program that will satisfy both environmentalists and athletes."

Now the grumbling came from everyone, athletes and environmentalists alike.

Barkey grabbed the microphone from Arnie. "Listen up," he screamed. "You're all gonna be happy. We're gonna have presentations by environmental folks and then comments by athletes including invitations to trash talk about the subjects. So everybody's going to have a chance to learn something. And keep in mind, all you athletes, you will get credit for attending."

Too Fat grabbed the mike from Chuck. "And maybe you assholes gonna learn somethin' new. I mean all you assholes, athletes and environmentees."

There were some hoots and catcalls as Too Fat handed the microphone back to Arnie.

Arnie went on, "Tomorrow morning at the first general session in the auditorium we will pass out new programs that will reflect the changes in both the meeting sessions and the social functions. In the meantime I beg you to finish registering and come to the opening cocktail party and buffet that will begin in about two hours. I apologize for

this misunderstanding, but I think we will all benefit and learn and enjoy this meeting. Thank you."

Arnie let out an audible sigh and jumped off
the chair. Oh man, he thought, at least we're still
alive. He turned to his colleagues, Pam, Melissa,
and Jordy. "Let's get to work finalizing the agenda
and make the required arrangements for our
modified social program."

They all turned, quickly thanked Barkey, Wilson, Gordon, and McCann, who were already being besieged with questions from some of their
athlete colleagues. The original committee scurried into Arnie's office and closed the door.

Monday morning brought new hope and new trep-
idation to Arnie and his small committee. The new
meeting programs were printed and a copy was
placed on each seat in the auditorium. In addition, piles of extra copies were evident at various
sites around the convention hall lobby. Arnie had
a slide presentation of the entire new program and
now planned to open the meeting by walking
everyone through it and answering any questions
from the audience regarding the program.

The cocktail party/buffet the night before had
been fairly successful. The evening started with the

athletes gathered around one of the two bars and the environmentalists at the other. The buffet as planned didn't stand a chance. The athletes had devoured every bit of food within fifteen minutes after the doors to the ballroom opened. The few environmentalists who attempted to get food before it was gone were so intimidated by the wide bodies surrounding the tables and the aggressiveness with which they devoured the shrimp, roast beef, clams, oysters, mini-sandwiches, and every other morsel on the table, that they stepped gingerly away and went to the quiet bar.

However, a few of the environmentalists, who for years shoveled food down at these affairs like they had not eaten in weeks, were not about to give up so easily. Mark Rhovosky, a professor of environmental science at Ohio State, in desperation, actually knocked "Big Tony" DiNardo aside with a flying block in the back and was able to catch three pieces of shrimp and two oysters that flew off Big Tony's plate as he stumbled forward. Tony knocked six or seven other athletes away from the buffet table as he tried to keep his balance. Pat O'Malley, another of Rhovosky's Ohio State colleagues, scooted in and grabbed four shrimp, three clams, and a piece of roast beef and scurried away to the bar before Big Tony or the other athletes could regroup.

Melissa, ignoring Arnie's hand-wringing comments about the food situation and their budget, instructed the hotel personnel to reload the buffet table. This was done and fortunately, the second feeding seemed to satiate the athletes, who once again congregated around one bar but left enough food to satisfy most of the environmentalists.

After a couple of hours, an interesting phenomenon occurred. The groups from the two bars started to mix. Some of the fairly inebriated athletes began to find some of the female environmentalists more attractive than they had at the beginning of the evening. And some of the somewhat inebriated female environmentalists began to find some of the athletes kind of cute and cuddly looking. Some of the environmentalists were sports fans and began to feel more comfortable conversing with the now-not-so-angry athletes. Overall, the evening went pretty well without any really unpleasant incidents. Everyone was wondering how Arnie and his group could modify the program to satisfy this strange group.

At 9:00 A.M. the auditorium was full. A few extra chairs had to be brought in since Too Fat McCann sat across three chairs and many of his fellow athletes required two chairs.

As Arnie waited for the crowd to get seated he

felt a tap on his shoulder. He turned and stood facing the beady eyes and stern face of Edmund Mundhill. "Ah . . . err . . . good morning, Mr. Mundhill."

"Good morning," snorted Mundhill. "How are you going to bail yourself out of this mess?" He stared at Arnie as if questioning his sanity. "You're going to have to be a magician to prevent this from being the biggest embarrassment in environmental history." His shoulders hunched up and he leaned forward into Arnie's face. "Do you realize that? What the press will do to us?"

"Look, Mr. Mundhill," Arnie replied in as steady and soft a voice that he could muster. "Just give us a chance. This meeting may be different than past meetings, but I think it will work. And look, we might be able to positively influence a bunch of people who are not professional environmentalists, and may not even be aware of the many problems that trash creates. Maybe they'll even become more environmentally friendly and be advocates for our work."

"Yeah, and maybe camels will fly," said Mundhill sourly.

"Look," said Arnie, "just have a seat and watch and wait. Hopefully, you'll be pleased."

Mundhill turned and began to move toward the seats. Then he swung his head back toward

Arnie. "I won't hold my breath waiting for success," he hissed and walked away. Arnie took a deep breath and felt a shiver.

Then Arnie stepped to the podium. He steadied himself by planting both hands on the lectern. "Good morning and welcome. I hope that everyone had a chance to mingle and meet people last night and enjoy themselves."

The audience sat silently staring at Arnie, waiting.

Arnie continued. "As you can see on this first slide, the new agenda shown on the left differs somewhat from the original agenda shown on the right. The first plenary session will now have two major presentations. The first, a thirty-minute presentation by Professor James Gribbs of the University of Michigan, entitled, 'Trash the World Over — Let's Recycle, Reduce and Reuse It.' This will be followed by a presentation by well-known retired basketball player and now sports commentator, Chuck Barkey. His presentation, also thirty minutes, is entitled, 'Trash Talk, It's Origins, Practice, and Environmental Impact.' Mr Barkey will address such environmentally relevant issues as, does trash talk lead to inappropriate urination and defecation? And, is spitting an environmentally harmful component of trash talk?

"After these two presentations and a fifteen-minute break, we will resume in the auditorium with two debates. The first will be between Professor Jerry Hood of the University of Iowa, and Professor Frank McDeil of the University of British Columbia. The subject is the transport of hazardous materials. Dr. Hood favors use of trucking and Dr. McDiel favors hauling by train. They will present and defend their positions. This will be followed by a debate, using trash talk as appropriate, between two hockey players, Ray McClaine of St Louis and Billy Barnes of Toronto. They will debate the reasons fans throw objects such as tampons and live octopuses on the ice during games. They will examine the psychology behind this, as well as cleanup and disposal difficulties, and the potential environmental impact. At the end of each thirty-minute debate, we will allow ten minutes for audience questions and comments. We will then adjourn to lunch.

"After lunch, we will resume with three parallel sessions. Session One, to be held in the Pelican room, is 'Sustainable Development without Burial by Trash.' Session Two, in the Seagull Room, is 'The State of Industrial Trash Compactors and Balers,' and Session Three, in the Manatee Room, is entitled, 'The Super Bowl and Excremental Overload: The Local Environmental Impact.' This will address the issue of beer sales and hot dog promotion increasing the level of defecation and urination of the one hundred thousand plus fans attending to a level that overloads the system, and endangers surrounding bodies of water. The question will be asked, 'Is this a real concern or just cosmetic?' Three speakers in each of these parallel sessions will present different outlooks on the issues. Audience questions and comments are encouraged.

"As you can see on the next slide, the parallel sessions end at four P.M. and you are encouraged to wander around the conference lobby and examine various vendor displays. There will be much equipment and materials on display, as well as many books of interest. We have also added the opportunity for participants to enter into one-on-one trash talk jousts with Sterling Parsche, Chuck Barkey, or Mo Robbins at booths set up in the vendor area. This will provide an opportunity for beginners to learn and practice, and for pros to improve.

"Tonight is a free night. There are lists of restaurants attached to your programs. Also, we have provided each of you with separate lists of theaters, libraries, art galleries, night clubs, and even go-go bars for those feeling more adventuresome. If any of you are looking for something not on the lists, see the people at the lobby desk for help. I really want to thank everyone who is willing to take on a topic at such short notice and to participate in a debate or make a presentation. I can't tell you how much the Planning Committee appreciates your help.

"I am now pleased to introduce my colleague, Jordy Gifford, who will chair the first session and introduce the speakers. Thank you."

There was tentative applause and a few whoops as Arnie stepped down and Jordy took the podium.

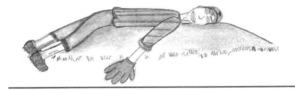

Day one was relatively successful. Professor Gribbs' presentation on 'Trash the World Over' went extremely well for the first twenty minutes, but then some of the athletes got a little bored.

Curt Shining, the only baseball player in the group shouted from the back row, "Enough shit. I don't want my dinner dishes made from somebody's garbage."

Before Professor Gribb could address the comment, Reggie Bright, a football player from Cleveland, shouted back at Shining, "Hey Curt, shut up and go back to sleep before we have another 'Shining moment'!"

All of the athletes and some of the environmentalists who followed major league baseball cheered and whooped. Bright's reference to a Shining moment was the result of an incident two weeks before that had brought Shining, an outstanding pitcher with Texas, to national sport's notoriety and to the injured reserve list, which was why he was available during baseball season to attend this meeting.

Shining was pitching a perfect game against Philadelphia. Texas led 2–0 in the top of the ninth. There were two outs and no Philadelphia batter had reached base. Shining was one out from a perfect game in front of his hometown crowd. He had two strikes and one ball on Hector Rivera, Philadelphia's all-star second baseman. The crowd was absolutely silent, although bursting with anticipation. Shining wound up and threw a high fastball right down the middle and Rivera connected solidly. Shining's mind was already on the celebration, and so he never reacted to avoid the line drive that came back like a bullet at the mound and hit him smack in the forehead. As Shining dropped like a stone, face down in a heap on the mound, the ball ricocheted in a slight arc right to Roberto Jessup, the Texas first baseman who was standing directly on the base and caught it for the final out. The crowd went wild, Texas players rushed from the dugout and from their positions on the field, but when they got to the pitcher's mound, they weren't sure what to do. A few patted the prone Shining on the back and congratulated him. Jessup lifted him up and held Shining erect, dancing around. Finally, he dropped Shining and the trainers picked him up and carried him to the dugout. Fortunately, some smelling salts restored his consciousness and tests revealed just a concussion, which would keep him out of the lineup for about two weeks. Shining only began to realize what happened after reading the many newspaper accounts of "another Shining moment" the next day.

After the brief outburst, Gribbs finished his presentation without further interruption.

Barkey's presentation went well. He started by providing a description of trash talk for the benefit of those environmentalists who were not familiar with the art form. He gained enthusiastic cheers from the athletes when he attributed the origin of trash talk to two college coaches. The late Woody Hayes, former football coach at Ohio State, and Bobby Knight, the basketball coach for many years at the University of Indiana, and more recently at Texas Tech. Barkey claimed that these two had proven that constant derogatory verbal comments to a player, whether on their team or on an opposing team, could significantly, negatively impact their game. They also proved that trash talk had no long-term harmful effects on the player since later praise always restored, and perhaps even improved, their ability to play.

Barkey also discussed potentially environmentally deleterious impacts of trash talk. He described one case of a designated hitter in the American League who became so irate at the remarks being made by the opposing catcher while the aforementioned batter was at bat that he threw down his bat, dropped his pants, and defecated on home plate. The catcher, crouched just behind the plate, promptly threw up, and the umpire, after retreating several feet toward the backstop, threw the batter out of the game. As it turned out, there were no scoopers or shovels to clean up the mess, and so the backup catcher's mitt was used. No one slid into home for the remainder of the game and most batters performed well below their usual batting average. The ousted batter was fined ten thousand dollars and suspended for three games, and the league imposed a requirement that shovel, pail, and mop be kept in the home team dugout for such emergencies. But, as far as anyone knew, they were never needed.

Although much spitting occurs in most pro sports, and there have been a few reports of football players being urinated on in the middle of a large pileup of players, Barkey concluded that, other than a brown spot or two on the real-grass football fields, there was no significant environmental impact from these activities, and that the activities were generally not provoked by trash talk.

The sessions that followed varied in their interest to the athletes. The debate on "Transportation of Hazardous Waste — Truck or Train" didn't seem to engender too much excitement, although some trash talk followed involving a few of the athletes.

Chuck Barkey chided Sterling Parsche, "Hey Parsche, you're waste, but you're not hazardous. Do you travel by truck or train?"

Parsche laughed. "Barkey, you were hazardous, but only to your own team. But you were merciful and retired."

Barkey laughed loudly as the athletes in the audience and even some of the environmentalists hooted. This type of interaction began to occur more regularly as the meeting went on and, on occasion, even an environmentalist took a shot at a trash talk comment.

One environmentalist shouted to Ray Mc-Claine and Billy Barnes at the end of their debate about why fans throw objects like live octopuses and tampons on the ice during hockey games. "Maybe they throw the octopuses to feed the hockey players."

There were some boos from the crowd and Barnes retorted, "Maybe, but if there were environmentalists on the ice, they could eat the tampons."

This led to more boos and hooting and whistling and everyone seemed to take the exchange in good spirit.

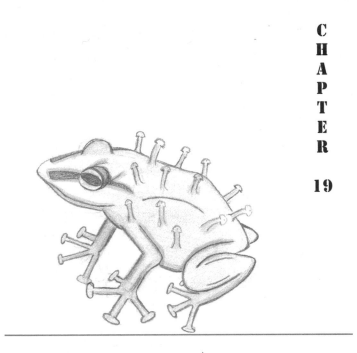

Arnie, Jordy, Pam, and Melissa circulated among the sessions during the day, and in the late afternoon they moved into the vendor display area. They each meandered through the group to get a feel for the atmosphere after a nearly completed first day of this strangely modified meeting. Most of the comments they overheard were pretty favorable, but some of the athletes and environmentalists were still ill at ease with each other. Jordy overheard one conversation among a group of environmentalists where someone said that watching the interactions at this meeting was like watching a football coach and a ballet director discuss the strategy for their respective upcoming events.

A surprisingly successful activity appeared to be the trash talk tutorials with Parsche, Barkey, and Robbins. Each booth was packed with a mixture of athletes and environmentalists and were exceptionally boisterous. Everyone seemed to be enjoying them.

One of the tutorials used the "mother insult" to demonstrate to the environmentalists some classic trash talk.

Robbins and Parsche illustrated.

Robbins: "Your mother's so fat, they crowned her 'Burger Queen'."

Parsche: "Your momma's so stupid, she thought manual labor was a Mexican hero."

Robbins: "Your momma's so old, I asked her to act her age and she dropped dead."

Parsche: "Your momma's so fat, when she got lost, they had to use all four sides of the milk carton."

Robbins: "Your momma's so dumb, she thought a quarterback was a refund."

Parsche: "Your momma's so dumb, it takes her two hours to watch *Sixty Minutes*."

Robbins: "Your momma's so old, she sat next to Jesus in the third grade."

Parsch: "Your momma's so ugly, she doesn't

have a receding hair line. That's her hair running away from her face."

The crowd laughed and enjoyed the banter. They applauded, hissed, boo'd, and hooted with each statement.

Nervously, Arnie craned his neck, trying to scan the faces in the crowd — especially the faces of the female environmentalists. Lots of them must be mothers for crying out loud. What if they — but no, even they were cracking up. At one point Arnie noticed Mundhill stopping to listen. But he quickly walked away wearing his standard frown. He appeared to be heading for the elevator. Hopefully, Arnie thought, going to his room.

The next tutorial run by Barkey and Wilson demonstrated the "ugly/stupid" insult approach to trash talk.

Barkey: "It's okay to be ugly, but you're abusing the privilege."

Wilson: "You are so stupid, you locked yourself in a bathroom and pissed your pants."

Barkey: "Act your age, not your IQ."

Wilson: "I would challenge you to a battle of wits, but I see you are totally unarmed."

Barkey: "You're so stupid, you stared at a box of juice because it said, 'concentrate'."

Wilson: "You're so ugly, your mom put a steak around your neck to get the dog to play with you."

Barkey: "You're so ugly, when you were born, the doctor smacked your mama."

Wilson: "Hey, man, who pissed in your test tube?"

Barkey: "If looks could kill, you would be the Terminator."

Wilson: "You're so dumb, you couldn't pass a blood test."

Barkey: "You're so stupid, you took the toilet paper to a crap game."

This tutorial session also engendered enthusiastic cheering from the audience. However, one female environmentalist in the audience seemed to be booing loudly at Barkey's remarks.

He looked her over and shouted, "Nice dress, lady. Some day it might be in style."

She quickly retorted, "I used to wear clothes like you until my dad got a job."

Everyone laughed and cheered and Chuck went over and shook her hand and bowed.

"Touché," he said. "Good job."

Another highlight of the meeting came on Wednesday morning at the opening presentation of the general session. Professor Jacques Dimone of Vancouver, Canada, presented his research on the impact of certain weed killers on the common northern frog, *Bufo Canadiensis*. It seems that exposure of the baby male frogs to a number of common weed killers induced the sprouting of multiple penises from various areas of their bodies, giving them a sort of miniature green porcupinish look.

Professor Dimone, in addition to being recognized as a brilliant scientist and an avid hockey fan, was also known to be fairly eccentric. It was quite common for Professor Dimone, who could lecture with the articulateness of an Oxford professor, to burst into a tirade in an exaggerated French Canadian accent and using multiple French Canadian colloquialisms, which is what he decided to use for his presentation to the environmentalists and athletes.

With a slide projected on the large screen of what looked like a green tennis ball with bulging eyes and numerous projectiles protruding from its body, Dimone began, "If you tink ders a problem wit trowin an octopus or two on de ice, just wait till dey start trowin dese little multi-penised buggers out der, eh!"

He then projected the next slide which was a close up of one of the projectiles.

There was a gasp from several members of the audience. It looked just like what it was, a penis. It was small, but not in perspective to the size of the frog. And it was bright green and very erect.

"Den what happens, all de female froggies in da area come hoppin to da arena to take advantage. Den we got ourselves a froggy orgy, eh."

With this statement, Dimone projected the next slide that set the audience atwitter with gasps, laughs, "Oh gods," and other utterances. What was pictured on the screen was one of the spiky tennis balls with five smaller and slightly lighter green tennis balls attached to five of the spikes.

Dimone continued. "We don't have no monogamy here. We got — serve all you can as long as der's a spare docking site. And dem frogs wit all dem penises, dey can screw demselves to death, eh. I measured heart rate on dese guys. It goes up to four times normal. Dat's like your heart beatin' four hundred times a minute."

A couple of "wows" from the audience.

"Now we got ourselves a big cleanup program. And if anyone tries to dispose of doz little dead green fornicatin factories, de little females attack dem, eh. So we got ourselves some hazardous waste, eh!"

Professor Dimone's presentation brought gasps from the environmentalists and cheers from the athletes.

Too Fat McCann shouted, "Spray me with some of that weed killer, quick!"

And another athlete retorted, "Hey Too Fat,

you already got one you don't know what to do with, and if you get more you'd have to sprout a whole bunch of additional hands too."

A lot of hoots and whistles followed.

One environmentalist asked Professor Dimone, "Do you think that we have to worry about our frogs in the United States? We still use some weed killers."

Professor Dimone retorted, "I doubt it. Down der in de states you're so up tight even your frogs wouldn't pop dem extra penises," and he laughed heartily at his own joke.

This garnered a cheer from most of the hockey players in the audience and even from a few of the Canadian environmentalists in attendance.

Arnie and his group breathed a collective sigh of relief at the end of the first day. Perhaps a disaster would be averted. Perhaps they might even have a modest success. Hell, confidence and enthusiasm were returning to the team. They might be seeing a roaring success after all. Life seemed good again for Arnie and his colleagues. At least for the time being.

Sarasota is a relatively reserved city. Its many tree-lined streets are populated with a multitude of art galleries, coffee houses, small cocktail lounges, theaters, novelty shops, and many very good restaurants. The few livelier bars in the area for the most part are not found downtown but rather along Route 41 both north and south of the city. Next to the Hyatt in Sarasota Quay, there is one night club that is modestly active on weekends but fairly quiet during the week. The city is also blessed with an outstanding opera house with its own resident company and the Van Wezel

Performing Arts Center, a thousand-plus-seat auditorium that hosts world-class entertainment nightly. In addition, the Sarasota area boasts some of the finest beaches in the world. North, along Longboat Key and south along Siesta Key, the talcum powder-like beaches are populated by sun lovers of every ilk; families, singles, seniors, the entire gamut find great pleasure in the blue-green water and on the white sand.

Arnie and his committee were much at ease during the planning period knowing that Sarasota could provide free-time recreational activities that would satisfy even the most demanding environmentalist. That was BTA — before the athletes! Now the collective feeling of the committee regarding recreation was anxiety. Since Arnie, Jordy, Melissa, and Pam had experienced the cautious elation of a surprisingly successful first meeting day, they were struck by the possibilities of the evening to come. Stomach acid flowed freely within the group and Jordy's Pepcid disappeared faster than sunflower seeds in a dugout or free recycled notepads at an environmentalist meeting.

Late the night before, after completing the revised meeting program, Arnie and Jordy had split up and visited several night spots to alert them to the possible number and size of patrons they could see for the next few nights. Although relatively rare, the few go-go joints were also visited and the message delivered. Arnie and Jordy sort of pictured themselves as the Paul Reveres of sleaze as they rode through the night delivering the news to all appropriate institutions.

Interestingly, what they considered to be news that would be cause for concern, was accepted with elation. Activity immediately heightened as bars and clubs scurried to place emergency orders for beer and liquor, and go-go joint managers placed calls to counterparts in Bradenton, St. Petersburg, Clearwater, and as far away as Tampa and Fort Myers in an attempt to round up more dancers to keep the action continuous. Monday morning traffic into the Sarasota area reached higher than usual levels with an abundance of beer trucks and stretch limousines, all with darkly tinted windows and packed with as many young ladies as would fit, all bound for the aspiring pleasure palaces of Sarasota. Numerous complaints to the police and letters to the editor of the *Sarasota Herald Tribune* followed from geriatric drivers who were intimidated and incensed by these foreign vehicles bearing down on them with horns blowing and obscenities being spewed from drivers and passengers. How dare they insist that the aging Sarasotan does not have the right to drive constantly in the left lane with the left turn signal blinking in case a decision is made to turn left. And young ladies in their low cut dresses hanging out the windows waving frantically at them to move aside and let them reach their destinations. It was a travesty!

All of Arnie's prayers and wishes and those of the other committee members could not stop Monday evening from arriving. At six o'clock the vendor area closed and the trash talk booths were emptied and everyone was on their own until nine o'clock the next morning.

Okay everybody. It's recreation time!

Maxwell Gordon met up with his old friend Mo Robbins and with Tony DiNardo in the lobby of the Ritz-Carlton with plans to go to dinner. Since Mo and Tony were living in Texas, and were major steak fans, the hotel concierge suggested they go to Ruth's Chris Restaurant, south on Route 41. Gordon had invited Chuck Barkey to join them, but he opted to eat at the Ritz-Carlton and have a look around the city afterward. Chuck also harbored some hope that Leona, the Ritz trainee, might be around and could spring loose for a little guided tour of the city. Not long after Robbins, Di-Nardo, and Gordon left, Barkey exited an elevator and entered the lobby, heading leisurely toward the front desk.

"Well, if it isn't Leona, my favorite Ritz-Carlton trainee in the whole world," said Chuck, with his best resistance-melting smile. "I am in need of a dining and touring partner, and the winning raffle ticket for this pleasure has your name on it — 'Leona the trainee'."

"Isn't that exciting, Mr. Barkey, but unfortunately, as you can see, I am presently gainfully employed. And, I'm afraid management would be sorely disappointed if I were to jump ship, so to speak, and accept this treasured prize that I have won," retorted Leona.

"Oh Leona, Miss Trainee rather, once the sun sets on Sarasota this evening it will never rise again if you don't find a way to honor your commitment as the grand prize winner," intoned Chuck.

"Oh, Mr. Barkey, I can tell that your attendance at the "Trash Talk" meeting, even after only one day, has markedly enhanced your ability to so melodiously deliver all this bullshit!" Leona answered.

Chuck howled and soon they were both having a vigorous laughing bout over the exchange. "Seriously," said Chuck, "don't you think the management would consider it an important part of your job to entertain important guests?"

"Oh yes," said Leona. "For important guests but —"

"Okay, okay," said Chuck. "No more trash talk for the day. Lessons over, even though I don't know who's the teacher and who's the student! When do you finish work?"

"Not until ten o'clock, pretty late."

"Well," said Chuck, "if it's not against the rules, why don't I meet you after I eat and you're finished and I can take you out for a snack."

"That sounds like a reasonable alternative to the grand prize. I'll be here at ten, but I can't stay out too late. I work the morning shift tomorrow."

"Hey little lady," said Chuck, "that sounds great. Don't forget, I have school in the morning. See you at ten." And Chuck headed off, smiling, toward the hotel restaurant.

John Delray, a quarterback with Kansas City, and Chuck Goodson, a defensive back with Pittsburgh, met Igor Federianov, a Russian hockey player with Detroit, and a few environmentalists at the Boat House Bar shortly after the end of the meeting sessions. After several drinks, the group decided to get some Japanese food at the restaurant across the street in Sarasota Quay, and planned to go from there to some of the go-go clubs along Route 41. The environmentalists were beginning to feel more like the athletes with every drink and by the time the teppanyaki dinner was devoured and three or four glasses of sake had been imbibed by each participant, a couple of five foot five environmentalists were feeling like the offensive tackles from the Baltimore Ravens.

When they hit The Saturn, a go-go bar on Route 41, the two little giants made a beeline for the bar and grabbed a couple of empty seats. They had what they considered to be two of the most beautiful women they had ever seen seated on the bar stools on either side of them. Joe Zedich from Syracuse, and Don D'Arma from Kalamazoo, were in heaven. This was nothing like the forests they stomped around in registering rare plant species. This was life the way the big guys lived it! Emboldened by the earlier martinis at the Boat House and the Japanese lightning they consumed at dinner, they dived into a few beers and a spirited conversation with the lovely lasses.

"Where you from?" asked Joe.

"We're from here," came the ladies' answer in unison.

"Whadda ya do?" said Don.

"Whadda ya mean?" the redhead next to Joe answered.

"Where do you work?" Don clarified.

"Look," said the blond next to Don, "you

gonna buy us a drink or you gonna keep grilling us with questions? What are you guys, detectives?"

"Yes," said Joe.

Simultaneously, Don said, "No."

"Do you two know each other?" asked blondie.

"Sure, sure" said Joe. "We're sort of plant detectives. Hey, what ya drinking?"

"I'll have a champagne cocktail," said redhead.

"Me too," said the blond.

"Hey, bartender," shouted Don, "bring these two lovely ladies champagne cocktails."

"Comin' up," said the bar man and was there with two drinks in no time.

"Here's lookin' at shya," said Joe with a slight slur as he lifted his glass and all four drank.

"What's a plant detective do?" asked redhead.

"Oh, it's exciting work," said Don. "We're out in the woods, you know. Among the wild animals. And we are searching for rare plants."

"What do you do with them when you find them?" asked blondie.

"Oh, we record them in our notebook and report back to the national society on our findings," answered Don.

The two women looked at each other wide eyed.

"Sure sounds exciting," said blondie, rolling her eyes.

"Oh yeah," said redhead. "How about another drink?"

"Oh, sure," said Joe. "Hey bartender, two more of the same for the ladies."

Both Joe and Don were beginning to have more problems with their speech, and the surroundings were beginning to look a little distorted too.

"What kind of wild animals are in the woods where you work? Where do you work?" asked blondie.

"Syracuse," said Joe.

"Kalamazoo," said Don.

"You look for plants in a zoo?" asked redhead, a puzzled look on her face.

"No, not in a zoo," said Don. "In Kalamazoo. That's a city in Michigan."

"Well, what kind of wild animals are in . . . Kala . . . my . . . er . . . whatever zoo you live in?" asked blondie

"Oh man, there are, uh, rabbits, chipmunks, squirrels, some deer. Somebody even saw a wolverine once."

"What the hell's a wolverine?" asked redhead, just as Chuck Goodsen appeared behind them.

"A wolverine, ladies, is a good lookin' defensive back from Pittsburgh. I went to college at the

University of Michigan. I am a wolverine. That was our school mascot."

John Delray appeared at his side. At six feet four and six feet five tall respectively, Chuck and John were an awesome contrast to Joe and Don.

"Well," said blondie, "I am a big wolverine fan. Let's go see how dangerous you can be." And with that she hopped off the barstool and took Chuck's hand.

Redhead dismounted her stool as well and slipped her arm around John.

As they began to walk away, blondie turned back and called, "Thanks for the drinks, guys. It was great talking with you."

"Yeah," yelled redhead. "See ya."

And they walked toward a booth in the back.

"Damn it," said Joe. "You scared them off with that animal talk. Hell, you Midwesterners don't know how to handle women."

"Hey," answered Don. "You're the guy who started that crap about detectives. I was gonna tell them we were pro athletes."

"What?" cried Joe, practically falling off his stool. "Pro athletes! What sport? Checkers?"

"Oh hell," said Don. "I'm not feeling that great anyway. Let's pay the bill and get out of here."

"Okay," responded Joe. "Hey bartender, can you bring us the bill, please."

"Comin' up," said the bartender as he totaled it and dropped it on the bar in front of them.

"I'll get this," said Joe as he picked up the small paper and looked at it as he reached for his wallet. "Holy shit!" he exclaimed as he stopped in mid-reach.

"What's the matter?" said Don.

"This must be somebody else's bill."

"Why?" said Don. "Let me see."

Joe's shaking hand held the one-hundred-forty dollar bill in front of Don's face.

Don removed his glasses to get a clearer look at such a close distance. "Jesus Christ," said Don. "You're right. This can't be ours."

"Bartender," Don called. "We got the wrong bill."

The bartender came down the bar, took the bill and looked at it. "Nope. It's right, and it is yours."

"How can that be?" whined Joe. "All we had was a couple of beers and the ladies had a couple of those cocktails."

"Yep," said the bartender. "Twenty-five dollars each for the champagne cocktails. That's one hundred dollars. Five dollars each for the beers. That's another twenty. So that's a hundred twenty. Five dollars cover charge for each of you makes it one thirty and taxes make it one hundred forty. And that don't include no tip."

A stunned silence followed.

"Yeah, okay," stammered Don as the bartender drifted away. "Holy shit, I only have forty dollars in cash."

"I've only got fifty," replied Joe. "Shit, we're fifty bucks short. I'll have to use my American Express card. If my wife ever looks at the Amex bill, I'm dead."

"I sure understand," said Don. "I have the same problem. My wife writes the checks for our bills. But I don't know what else to do."

"Well," said Joe, "we could just leave some money under the check and take off. Hell, it's a rip-off and I wouldn't feel we were really cheating anybody if we leave forty apiece and just leave. That's fair enough."

They each put forty dollars on the bar, pushed the money together, covered it with the bar tab, and, as nonchalantly as they could, staggered toward the door.

As they reached the door, the giant bouncer, after a nod over their heads toward the bar, stepped in front of them. "I think the bartender wants to talk with you fellows," he said in a gravelly voice as he put his arm on the shoulders of the two escaping scientists and led them toward an office behind the end of the bar.

Arnie and Jordy were out on a recreation patrol, driving around town on the lookout for any trouble when they spotted the police car parked in front of the Saturn and two policemen entering the establishment.

"Uh-oh," said Arnie as he pulled the car into a vacant spot across the street from the club. "We better take a look and make sure that none of our group has a problem."

"Yes," replied Jordy. I think you're right — to be on the safe side."

They entered the bar just in time to see the two policemen follow a man in a white apron and two familiar figures into a room at the end of the bar.

"Damn," said Arnie, "those are a couple environmentalists from the meeting. I know that one guy is from Syracuse."

"We better see what's going on," said Jordy.

"Yeah," said Arnie as they approached the now closed door and knocked.

The door was opened slightly by the bartender, who looked out at Arnie and Jordy. "Yeah?" he said.

"Look, we're with the Sarasota Environmentalist Society," said Arnie. "We have a meeting in the city, and we just saw two of our members go into that room with you. Is there a problem?"

"Not yours," said the bartender and closed the door.

Arnie knocked again and the door opened wider.

"I told you, it's not your problem," said the bartender but one of the police officers looked out and recognized Arnie from all of the discussions that Arnie had with the police in preparing for the meeting.

"Let them in," said the officer. "They're officials with the Environmentalist Society, and these guys claim to be attending their meeting."

Arnie and Jordy squeezed past the bartender and into the room.

"Thank God," said Joe. "Arnie, we need some help. We got ripped off."

"They tried to rip me off," shouted the bartender.

"Wait! Wait!" interrupted the police officer.

"You," and he pointed at Joe, "tell your story so we can all hear it, and remain calm while you're telling it."

Joe began, and with Don's help, they got through their version.

The bartender began to say something in response, but he was stopped by the police officer who put up his hand, palm out toward the bartender.

"Look," said the cop, "I'm not a big fan of what goes on here with the bar girls and the drink rip offs. But it's not illegal or so it seems," and he looked at Arnie. "Your friends owe the place sixty dollars."

As Arnie turned toward Joe and Don, Don said, "We're willing to pay for it but we don't have that much cash and if I put it on my credit card and my wife sees the statement, I'm dead."

"Me too," said Joe.

"Hey look," said Arnie as he reached for his wallet and looked at the bartender. "If I pay the rest of this bill, will you let these guys go?"

"Yeah," said the bartender. "I ain't lookin' to bust their chops or put them in jail. I just want my money."

"Is that okay?" Arnie asked the officer.

"Sure, just so everybody's happy," said the cop.

Arnie pulled out sixty dollars and handed it to the bartender.

"I guess I don't get a tip, huh?"

"I'll give you a tip," said one of the cops. "Tell your bar girls to pick on someone their own size."

The cops chuckled and left, followed closely by Arnie, Jordy, and their two escapees. Outside, Don and Joe, who had sobered up significantly from the trauma, couldn't thank Arnie and Jordy enough.

"You saved us," exclaimed Don. "Jesus, if a report had somehow gotten back to my wife or if they would have called her and told her I was in jail, I'd never hear the end of it.

"Well," said Jordy, "everything is okay now. We're going to drive you back to your hotel. Hopefully you'll stick to art galleries for the rest of the meeting."

They all laughed weakly as they got into Arnie's car.

At ten o'clock Chuck Barkey was back at the front desk of the Ritz-Carlton.

"Well, Leona, it's the witching hour, ten o'-clock, and your Prince Charming is here to take you to the royal ball."

"Well, Prince," said Leona, "I accept an offer of a one-hour walk around the city, topped off by one glass of wine, and then off I go to bed. Alone! Is that acceptable your highness, my prince?"

"I am afraid I am forced to accept this lean but promising offer in lieu of even greater charms. But the city awaits."

Leona bid goodbye to her fellow workers and arm in arm she and Chuck left the hotel.

When Leona awoke for work early the next morning, she once again marveled at the wonderful time she had the night before, and at what a gentleman Chuck Barkey had been. They walked around town in the moonlight and had a drink at the Silver Cricket before Chuck dropped her at her apartment on Orange Avenue. He had made no pass — just a slight peck on the cheek — and said good night. And he had been a very interesting and entertaining conversationalist. Leona was impressed at Barkey's knowledge of art and the pleasure he got from looking in the art gallery windows along Palm Avenue. And he also regaled her with some of the dishes he prepared in his kitchen.

Chuck told her he started cooking about ten years earlier. He had never cooked before that. He felt that he had eaten out so much and in so many places that he developed a feel for what would taste good and what ingedients went well together. He said he considered himself the "Monet" of the kitchen — a food impressionist, not a cook. When Leona had asked him if he might cook — or create as he considered it — for her someday, he said absolutely. But warned her, "Since I never use a recipe, I can't promise that I can repeat anything that I have prepared to be just the same the next time, and every meal is an experiment, so we could end up at a restaurant."

Leona told him that he couldn't frighten her off so easily and some day she would be there to collect her meal – or work of art. She guessed that the questionable reputation of many pro athletes must be very exaggerated. She had certainly become a fan of Chuck Barkey. She decided that his reputation as a very eigible bachelor was well deserved.

After dropping Joe and Don off at the Hyatt, Arnie and Jordy took another swing through the city and up and down a few miles of Route 41, and were relieved to find nothing unusual. They saw some small groups of meeting attendees that they recognized walking casually back toward the hotels. Probably coming from late dinners or one of the bars, but seemingly enjoying themselves. With a sigh of relief, Arnie dropped Jordy at his car in the Hyatt parking lot and took off for home.

On Tuesday morning a strange phenomenon occurred. A sizeable number of local residents
showed up and requested single-day registration.
They had read a small article on the front page of
the *Sarasota Herald Tribune* that morning describing the meeting and the misunderstanding. It read
in part,

> It appears the meeting of the Na-
> tional Environmentalist Society be-
> ing held at our city's Hyatt Hotel
> drew some unexpected attendees.
> The theme, "Trash Talk," was misin-

terpreted, and a sizable number of very large people — professional athletes — showed up to fulfill their newly imposed educational requirement. When they found out the trash being talked about was real, sloppy, soggy garbage and not the art of insult, they were not happy. But it seems that a compromise has been reached between organizers and athletes and a new, imaginative program was worked out. This meeting could be worth the price of admission.

The locals that came to observe boosted the daily attendance by another seventy-three, and the organizers happily accepted their fees, gave them programs, and squeezed more chairs into the back of the auditorium. This meeting was becoming a real money maker. Arnie began to hope that they might all still have jobs afterward. But he wasn't ready to bet on it.

The general session of the meeting opened with a talk by Professor Sue Greber of Harvard. Greber grew up in Pennsylvania, where she loved to ski, hike, ride bicycles and even a motorcycle, but had to take a break from these activities when she went off to school. She had impressive academic credentials. Undergraduate degree from Wellesley, doctorate in environmental science from UCLA, and a three-year post-doctoral stint at Yale, where she studied environmental ethics. She was hired at Harvard as an assistant professor of environmental studies, and had been promoted to associate professor after four years, which put her on the tenure-track.

Now five years later, she was a full professor, with tenure, at Harvard and was able to renew some of her old interests. Of course she had never stopped skiing, but found more time for it in the last five years. She also bought a motorcycle and rode with several groups, even an occasional outing with the Hells Angels.

Professor Greber, a small, frail-looking dark-haired woman, was a legend on the ski slopes of New England. She was so incensed by the degree of littering on ski mountains, she had become a one-woman police force of the ski resorts and punisher of the litterers. Professor Greber, an excellent skier, dressed in a Harvard crimson ski outfit and her white ski cap with a red 'H' on the front would scour the slopes looking for litterers. When she spotted someone dropping a tissue or a candy or chewing gum wrapper or other waste on the snow, she would veer off her course, and careening up behind the perpetrator, the wiry little avenger would whack the misbehaver with her ski pole on the back of their calf just above their ski boot.

This caused the environmental criminal to drop in his or her tracks, clutching at the back of their leg and writhing around with the stinging pain.

Professor Greber would continue on her way shouting, "Don't be a litterbug," and, as she quickly skied away, the sorrowful victim would see the large white 'H' on the back of her crimson outfit. The injury she imposed was temporary, and left the skier with a black-and-blue welt, but able to finish their ski day. They left with no lasting effect other than a paranoia about ever dropping another bit of anything on a ski slope. Although there had been periodic reports to the ski resort managers about Dr. Greber, who had come to be referred to as the "Crimson Scourge," nothing was ever done, since the noticeably cleaner slopes were a real benefit. Periodically you would hear groups of skiers talking about the "red and white flash," the "red and white slasher," the "midget marauder," or the "cleanliness nut." And most skiers on the slopes of Vermont, New Hampshire, and Maine were reluctant to throw away trash anywhere but in a container for fear the little lady in crimson with ski pole flailing would come out of nowhere and punish them.

Professor Greber was chairing a session on "Recreational Trash," and was acting as the lead-off speaker with the topic, "Problems of Trash on the Ski Slopes." In her presentation, she discussed the most common types of ski slope litter: tissue papers, paper coffee cups, soft drink and beer cans, cigarette butts, an occasional condom, and other odds and ends. She described some accidents caused by skiers running over these types of items, such as the skier who went out of control, hit a tree, and broke his arm when an old condom stuck to the bottom of his ski. Professor Greber also alluded to some of her corrective actions aimed at the perpetrators, and encouraged environmentalist skiers to take up the cause in similar fashion.

Dr. Greber's presentation was quite well received and she was particularly praised by some of the hockey players in the audience who thought that the "calf whack" was a great weapon for the skiing environmentalist.

Through the remainder of the day, the meeting seemed to proceed smoothly. Major speakers, panel participants, and workshop debaters all seemed to get into the rhythm of the mixed-audience requirements. Athletes started to ask questions about environmental issues and comment on issues related to environmental causes that bothered them. Whereas they could understand and support to some extent concerns such as excess chemical use on golf courses and the potential runoff into streams, lakes, and oceans, they had little sympathy for extremists who argued that killing real grass on football and baseball fields and cutting down trees to supply wood for basketball courts and baseball bats was immoral. Many of the environmentalists who had not previously had much interest in professional sports found themselves gaining interest as they talked with the athletes at breaks and at the social events.

At the end of the day's sessions, most participants left the lecture hall and drifted into the adjoining convention lobby to explore the exhibits. Some of the fitness-oriented attendees went off to change into workout clothes and then to the fitness center or out into the fresh air for a jog. A few who were not interested in more business or in fitness headed to the bar for an early start.

Randy Wilson and Bill Gladly were looking around the exhibit hall when they saw a group gathered near a line of portable toilets that were on display. There was a lot of cheering and laughing, and so they decided to go and see what was going on. When they got to the group they heard some shouting and arguing.

"What's going on?" asked Bill of two men at the back edge of the crowd.

One of the men explained. "Oh, these guys who are the manufacturers' representatives for these different porta toilets, or whatever they're called, have gotten into a debate as to which product has the best name. They started out arguing about who had the best product, but I think they realized that there's really no difference so now they're onto the names."

"Sounds wild," said Wilson with a bit of sarcasm in his tone, as they edged closer to the combatants.

"Mr. John! That's a shit name," said one of the debaters.

"That's exactly what it's supposed to be. A shit name," said the man in front of the Mr. John. "At least it doesn't look like a piece of shit like your Johnny Boy!"

"My Johnny Boy looks great. Red, white, and blue is a great color scheme. Easy to find and patriotic," said the Johnny Boy representative.

"Yeah," said Mr. John, "People don't know whether to shit in it or salute it!"

"Hey guys," said a third person. "My product,

Porta Pottie, is the best. It's name is self-explanatory. No one will mistake it for a phone booth."

"Jesus," said Johnny Boy. "Who uses these, two-year-olds? Porta Pottie? Why not make it adult, like Porta Crapper, then it would be self-explanatory."

"Wait, wait," cried a fourth man with a pronounced British accent. "Our Porta Loo has been the classiest product, but for the American market, we are launching a product with a more appropriate name but still with an English presence. We're calling it the Poop Palace!"

A cheer went up from the crowd.

Someone hollered, "Let's go to the Poop Palace," and the crowd started a chant. "Poop Palace, Poop Palace, let's go to the Poop Palace and we'll have a jolly good time."

Gladly looked at Wilson. "Man, these environmental people are weird. Let's go get a beer."

"I'm with you," said Wilson. "Off to the Poop Palace! You can sit on the Queen's throne!" And off they went chuckling.

Billy Barnes found Professor Greber at the Boat House bar having a beer after the sessions ended.

"Hi, Professor Greber," said Billy. "I'm Billy Barnes. I'm a hockey player with Toronto. I really enjoyed your presentation today. With that calf whack you oughta think of playing hockey. You could be tough."

Professor Greber chuckled. "Call me Sue or Grebs. That professor crap is for the classroom. You want a beer, Billy? Grab a stool."

"Yeah, thanks. I'll take a Molson," said Billy.

"One Molson for my buddy here and another Sam Adams for me," Greber called to the bartender.

"So, what do you think of the meeting, Billy? A little strange, huh?"

"Yeah, I was sort of pissed, er, upset rather, excuse me, when it started, with all the mix-up and all, but it's actually gotten pretty interesting and sort of fun. I never thought that much about all the shit, er, junk I mean, excuse me, that gets tossed on the ski runs. Its bad enough with what those assholes, er, excuse me, fans, throw on the ice at our hockey games. I almost busted my ass, er, almost took a bad fall, excuse me, the other night when I ran over a fuckin', I mean a damn, excuse me, belt that somebody threw on the ice."

"Hey, Billy," said Greber. "Let's make a deal. You use whatever language you want and don't litter our conversation with all those fucking 'excuse me's.' Okay?"

"Hey, I like that, doc, er, Sue, Grebs. Oh shit, excuse me"

They both broke up with laughter.

"I really like you, Grebs."

"I like you too, Billy. Let's get the hell out of here and go get some dinner. I'm starved. Maybe we can figure out how to clean up the world over some food. By the way, do you ski?"

And with that she slid off the stool, put a twenty dollar bill on the bar, slid her arm into Billy's, and off they went to find a restaurant.

Ginnie Chester, an environmental scientist working for General Motors with an interest in reducing auto emissions, went to dinner Tuesday with Andre Webster, the all-pro wide receiver from the Cleveland Browns. Andre had been questioning Ginnie at an earlier coffee break about what she did at General Motors. He was fascinated at her approaches to studying auto emissions. Andre had grown up in Birmingham, Alabama, in a house that was next door to an auto repair shop. He was good friends with the son of the shop's owner and spent a lot of time watching the boy's father and the other employees repairing cars. Andre had learned quite a bit and impressed Ginnie with his knowledge of automobile engines. She was even more impressed when she learned that he had graduated from Georgia Tech with a degree in mechanical engineering, and accomplished that while starting at wide receiver for the Tech football team for four years. Although football dominated his life these days, he was certain that in the future when his football career ended he would get to his other love, engineering. Ginnie grew up in Grand Rapids, Michigan, with four brothers so she had more than a passing knowledge of football. During her years at the University of Michigan, where she got her engineering degree, she was an avid football fan and continued to attend a couple of Michigan games every year since graduation.

The two hit it off so well at the coffee break that Andre had asked Ginnie to have dinner at Café L'Europa, a restaurant that Andre was told by the hotel concierge was one of the best in the area. The two took a taxi to the restaurant, which was about two miles from the hotel in a popular tourist area, St. Armand's Circle. The dinner was outstanding, and Ginnie and Andre immensely enjoyed each others' company. By the time they returned to the hotel, they had exchanged addresses and phone numbers and Andre invited Ginnie to a couple of Browns home games in Cleveland, as well as to their game against the Lions in Detroit. Ginny was thrilled. Andre even offered to send her extra tickets for her brothers who lived in the Detroit area.

* * *

Tony DiNardo and Bernie McCann went to dinner on Tuesday at Zaks, a relatively new steakhouse in Sarasota. They were joined by four environmentalists, two men and two women. Too Fat had the group totally entertained with his description of his parasailing experience. They were laughing so hard they were afraid of disturbing the other patrons in the rather small restaurant. However, many of the others overheard Too Fat's story and were laughing too. Bill Radcliffe, one of the environmentalists at the table then informed the group that his hobby was flying ultralights, the little paper-winged aircraft with a motor about the size of a lawnmower engine. He described the beauty of soaring around alone several hundred feet in the air with great views of the countryside.

Everyone looked at Too Fat, whose eyes were as wide as saucers, and as they started to laugh, DiNardo said, "McCann, don't even think about it. You would need a jet engine, and even with that you would probably hit the ground like a big meteor."

The group was in tears with laughter.

"Hey," replied Too Fat, "you don't have no worries about me. I ain't leavin' Mother Earth for nothin' except to fly in a plane with four engines and two pilots, and even then only when I absolutely have to do it."

Everyone howled.

Seriously though," said Radcliffe, "the important thing about ultralights is that they are a step in the direction of less-polluting travel, and they also can relieve some of the traffic congestion."

The group all agreed with that aspect of ultralight flight, but also insisted that a safer solution was required. Individual transporters that are less or non-polluting and don't crowd the roads as much certainly could be an attractive approach.

This idea fascinated Too Fat. "Hey guys, maybe I could get one of them new things that look like the front end of a scooter and are balanced when you stand on them."

"You mean a Segway," said Radcliffe. "That's exactly the type of transporter that I'm talking about.

"Yeah," said McCann. "A Segway. It goes on the ground, not in the water or up in the air."

"Yeah," said DiNardo, "but if you tried it, they'd have to put eighteen-wheeler tires on it and call it 'Gangway' or 'Get Outta the Way'!"

Everyone laughed, even Too Fat.

C
H
A
P
T
E
R

24

Arnie, Melissa, Jordy, and Pam were between relief and pure joy by Wednesday as they saw the relationship among the attendees become friendlier and the interactions more spontaneous.

"Just two more evening functions and we'll be home free," said Melissa. "I'm not worried anymore about the meeting itself. We got another forty-two locals today. Our attendance is incredible. Everyone seems to be getting along. But I still get goose bumps as we approach the social functions. Once the group gets into cocktails, things seem to change."

"Yeah," said Jordy, "after a few cocktails the

environmental folks only differ from the athletes in size, not in behavior."

"Are you kidding?" chimed in Pam. "The athletes are better behaved. These environmentalists are going crazy. They drink more, and seem like they want to experience the life of a pro athlete."

"You're right," said Arnie. "At least the sports guys seem to be able to handle the liquor. Some of our folks are experiencing hangovers for the first time in their life. I've been thinking that the influence of those hangovers may be the only thing that keeps them from going totally nuts when they get out on the town."

"Well, as I said, only two more nights," repeated Melissa. "Even old Mundhill seems to be all right. At least he hasn't said anything more."

"Maybe he will even crack a smile, but that's not likely," said Arnie. "Only two more nights, but I would hate to be known as the leader of the group that destroyed the Van Wezel or the Hyatt."

"You know, Arnie," said Jordy, "I'm not too worried about the closing banquet Thursday here at the hotel. At least many of the folks only need to make it upstairs to their room afterward. And the hotel has reasonable security."

"That's true," said Arnie. "But the hotel security wouldn't fare well against a bunch of three-hundred-pound pro athletes."

"You're right," said Jordy, "but I'm more concerned that the environmentalists will go nuts, and the reason I'm worried about the Van Wezel is that their security people are all about eighty-five-years-old!"

"Perhaps," said Arnie, "we should hire some of our own security for tonight. I'll check with the management at Van Wezel and see if they mind. I hope that I don't scare the daylights out of them. I don't want them to think we're going to have a riot."

A call to the Van Wezel resulted in an agreement that the performing center would have their entire security force on duty, but they preferred no outside help. They were confident in their people.

Evening approached, and the buses pulled up at the Hyatt for the short trip to the Van Wezel. The attendees had been advised to dine early, and to be ready to leave for the theater at 7:30 P.M. in time to get seated for the show, which was to begin at 8. Although Jordy urged the group to use the buses, there were many who expressed a desire to walk the short distance. At about 7:15, the four buses began making trips to the Van Wezel, dropping off people and coming back for more. The sidewalks between the Hyatt and the Center, just a couple blocks away, were crowded with a stream of meeting attendees, some very large and some quite small, but all seemingly in a jovial state of mind. A few of the walkers seemed to trace a zig-zagging path as they headed north from the hotel, the victims of pre-dinner, dinner, and post-dinner beverages.

The entrance to the Van Wezel was jammed. Most of the meeting attendees had purchased tickets to see Kenny Rogers. He was popular with all the attendees, whether athlete or environmentalist.

As the group made their way past the ticket collectors and into the lobby of the performing arts center, a quite elderly ticket taker with a pronounced hearing deficit thought he heard someone say, "There's Fat," as he pointed to another line. He looked over in the direction the man pointed, and spotted Too Fat McCann in another line along with Chuck Barkey. The old gent couldn't believe his eyes. He bolted from his ticket collection position toward Too Fat, leaving a long line of entrants standing there momentarily and then, as they realized they were in a dead-end line, struggling to merge with the adjacent line where there was someone taking tickets.

The tall, thin, white-haired, frail-looking, ticket taker pushed his way through the throng of people toward Too Fat and Chuck. Along the way he grabbed a program from one of the piles and, breathing heavily — almost gasping for air and waving the program and a pen in the air — he half lunged, half stumbled into the line in front of McCann and Barkey. In an excited, breathless voice he said to McCann, "Fats, Fats, may I have your autograph?"

McCann, stumbling back — the old gent was standing so close — said, "Certainly, man, anytime," and began to sign the program.

"You wouldn't consider one chorus of 'Blueberry Hill' would you?" wheezed the old man while Bernie was signing.

"What?" McCann blinked.

" 'Blueberry Hill.' C'mon just a little," urged the man.

Barkey laughed so loud that the burst caused the old guy to drop the autographed program that Too Fat had just handed back.

"Holy shit," cried Barkey. "He thinks you're Fats Domino! Come on Fats, just a few bars," choked Barkey almost on the ground with laughter.

Barkey started, "I found my thrill" as McCann, stammering, began to try to explain to the elderly gentleman, who had retrieved his signed program and was now joyously waving it in the air, that he was Too Fat McCann, a football player and not the old singer, Fats Domino.

"Nah Fats, you can't fool me," said the elderly ticket collector, "I always been a big fan of yours." But then, in a loud whisper he said as he got very close, "I understand, Fats. You'd be mobbed if you got recognized by this big crowd. Have a good time in the show. I won't tell no one that you're here. Thanks for the autograph." And with that, he turned spryly and made his way back toward his post.

Chuck could hardly contain himself. He was doubled over with laughter as he tried to sing, "I found my thrill on blue . . ."

But he got no farther before he dropped on his hands and knees with laughter.

Too Fat just looked down at him, shaking his head.

The 500-plus meeting attendees that were flooding into the auditorium took up a significant portion of the seating. The theater reverberated with the chatter and laughter and loud calls from one section to another as people made their way to their seats. Many attendees made a quick stop at the refreshment area or the bar in the lobby as they headed into the auditorium.

Arnie and his group stood in the lobby of the Van Wezel observing the arrivals. They were a little concerned about the state of sobriety of a few and the hints of whiskey and beer bottles in the pockets of others.

"Just get me through this night," Arnie prayed silently.

At five after eight, with everyone seated, the lights dimmed, a spotlight highlighted an announcer as he walked on stage, microphone in hand. "On behalf of the Sarasota Arts Council and the Van Wezel Performing Arts Center, I would like to welcome you to a night with Kenny Rogers!"

A roar went up from the audience. Thunderous applause filled the auditorium.

The announcer held up his free hand in a gesture to quiet the crowd, and he went on. "I would like to acknowledge the presence in the audience this evening of attendees at a very important meeting in Sarasota this week, the National Environmentalist Society."

Once again the auditorium shook with applause and hoots, primarily from Arnie's strange army of attendees. This applause lasted even longer than the initial burst. Arnie's anxiety level increased significantly. This exaggerated enthusiasm did not bode well for an orderly evening.

Trouble began with the next announcement.

The announcer began, "Before we introduce Kenny, we have an opening act I think that you will enjoy —"

But before he got any further, someone in the audience shouted, "No. We want Kenny!"

And this was followed by a chorus of, "We want Kenny! No other act. No opening act!"

The announcer tried to regain control, pleading for patience and a willingness to wait a short time for Kenny Rogers and to give the opening act a break. Some in the audience, who were not part of Arnie's meeting, and were generally very senior citizens, began to shout at the environmentalists to quiet down and show some respect for the opening performers.

A few shouting matches between members of the two groups ensued, but finally died down and the announcer jumped in. "I'd like you to give a big round of applause for a new young rock group from the Sarasota area, The Mad Dogs! Let's put our hands together and welcome these young gents."

The curtain opened to reveal six shaggy looking young men, four black and two white, with long scraggly hair and outfits that looked like they had accidentally landed on the performers during a wind storm. The group immediately broke into their repertoire with an ear-piercing volume of guitars, drum, trumpet, and saxophone and a lead vocalist who proceeded to scream a steady stream of nonunderstandable words. Additional screaming was provided by the rest of the group as backup.

Then the trouble got worse.

The entire audience, environmentalists and athletes, meeting attendees and senior Sarasotans, all began shouting.

"Get them off the stage."

"They're terrible."

"They're ruining my hearing aid."

"Stop! Stop!"

Then someone threw a handful of peanuts at the group. Next, a wine cork bounced off the singer and candy bars bounced on the stage. At that point the curtain quickly closed and the horrible sound of the group was muffled and then stopped.

But the screaming and shouting of the audience got worse.

After a minute or so — although it seemed forever — the audience turmoil was brought to a sudden halt when Kenny Rogers himself, guitar in hand, stepped out from behind the curtain. The audience became totally silent for a few seconds, and then burst into wild applause and cheering.

"My, oh my," said Kenny in his slight drawl, "you are a cranky audience. Why I almost got hit with a set of false teeth as I stepped onto the stage."

More cheering ensued.

Kenny held up his hands. "Okay. Okay. Hold on."

The audience quieted.

"You sure are a demanding audience. I'm almost afraid to perform."

Additional cheering and applause came from the audience.

"But I'll go ahead," said Kenny. "Those poor young fellas you chased away will get a little more practice then they'll do okay, but another time."

"I'm afraid I am going to have to do a bit of a solo till they clean up the stage and I can bring on my group. So I'll tell you what, let's put that energy you all have to some productive use. Come on and pitch in and we'll do one of the old favorites together. So put those hands together and get those strong voices going as we, together, do 'Lucille'."

The audience went wild as Kenny started to strum his guitar. Thanks to his willingness and stamina, Rogers provided a non-stop two hours of music, the last hour and a half accompanied by his band and backup singers who were finally able to take the stage. Kenny, during his solo half hour did "Lucille" and then "The Gambler" — twice. Each time the crowd enthusiastically sang along. After he was joined by the rest of the band they did a few of their lesser known songs like "Buy Me a Rose,"

"Loving Arms," "Let It Be Me," and "The Kind of Fool Love Makes." It looked like they were ending at this point, but incredible, prolonged applause encouraged the group to go on with "When a Man Loves a Woman," "My Funny Valentine," "Love Will Turn You Around," and "Through the Years." The crowd was totally mesmerized and very appreciative, cheering wildly at the end of each song and sometimes singing along or clapping to the rhythms.

During his last song, Kenny took his guitar and, still singing, left the stage and stepped down into the audience. He left the music to his band and backup group and began shaking hands as he walked through rows of spectators. He spoke with many of the athletes that he recognized but also took time to chat briefly with some environmentalists and other members of the audience. After a couple of songs he returned to the stage for a brief finale. A long, loud, standing ovation at the end resulted in two encore songs before the curtain closed. The crowd once again requested "Lucille" and "The Gambler" and they were not disappointed.

A very energized audience left the auditorium, many humming or singing their favorite Kenny Rogers tune. The meeting attendees headed back toward the hotels, some by bus and many by foot. Spirits were high but none were higher than those of Arnie and his committee. Another day complete and no major problems.

Pam said, "Thank God. Hopefully we are over the hump. Tomorrow night is the banquet and that will keep most of the people in the Hyatt."

"Yes," said Jordy, "that should be a little more controllable. No outsiders."

"Yes," replied Arnie, "but I won't breathe easily until Friday morning when they're all checked out of the hotel."

"Well," Melissa said, "I'll breathe more easily when I get the feeling that every meeting attendee has left Sarasota and is on their way home!"

"Yeah," I know what you mean," said Jordy, and they all chuckled.

"Well, folks," said Arnie, "go home and get some rest. Tomorrow is a long day and we have to be really alert at the banquet to make sure everyone stays happy and has a good time. So take your social host or hostess pill in the morning and be ready to shine. Good night. See you in the morning."

Good nights were expressed all around and they each headed for their cars.

The meeting sessions on Thursday flowed as well as the previous day, and everyone seemed to be pleased. The presentations appeared to hold the mixed audience's interest. Even Ed Mundhill had moved to a front row seat next to Rama Schriff, but the two didn't say much to each other. A presentation by Nathan Adamson, an environmental engineer from a cosmetic company in California, described his work to reduce the non-hazardous waste at his company's facility. The effort led to the replacement of a waste/scrap shredder with a compactor and a more aggressive recycling program.

Bill Gladly asked Adamson if a lot of cosmetics contained fragrances that were derived from bugs and if bug parts were in their waste stream.

Before Adamson could answer, Tony DiNardo shouted, "Maybe you basketball players should stop using makeup if you're scared of bugs."

Gladly retorted, as the audience applauded, "I was asking about the bug parts in the waste stream because I thought that it could be turned into a product especially for football players."

This led to some additional applause, and then Adamson assured everyone that their cosmetics didn't contain any bug juice or bug parts so all athletes could be comfortable with their makeup and cologne.

This got applause from both athletes and environmentalists.

Fred Sawyer, an engineer with a Florida citrus juice company, reported on the replacement of filter bags with a filter press to improve the quality of wastewater discharged from the company plant.

Dale Bowl of the University of Florida, followed Sawyer's presentation with a commentary on the impact of wastewater on fish life in the Florida waterways and bays. He was very complimentary of the work done by Sawyer and his company. Bowl also talked about the "Red Tide" and what little was known about why this algae invaded the Florida shorelines so frequently. He also urged more research into possible preventive measures. He implied that the fishing industry, which suffered greatly as the fish were killed by this intruder, might be willing to fund some of the research. Some environmentalists from coastal states seemed keenly interested in this information and started a buzz.

An employee of the Sierra Club provided an impassioned plea for support of regulations to reduce or eliminate logging in federally owned forests, arguing that the value of the timber produced was miniscule compared with the environmental damage caused by the harvest. The speaker also hypothesized that bare areas in the parks encouraged littering and would turn these areas into "veritable trash dumps."

This led to some lively interchanges between the speaker and audience members, some of whom favored the ban and others, who thought that logging was valuable both commercially and as a way to refresh the forest. Some suggested that rapid replanting would prevent the "trash dump" concern.

And then, of course there were many presentations on global warming and its effect on trash disposal. Some speakers claimed that elevated temperatures would hasten the degradation of trash at disposal sites and shorten the duration of the unpleasant odors caused by the decaying trash. Others argued the opposite. That is, the enhanced decay would cause more odor and greater danger of overgrowth of bacteria and other parasites, creating a health hazard. One speaker claimed that global warming would have absolutely no impact on any aspect of the environment or on the trash to which the environment is exposed.

This debate led the chairperson of the session, Sylvia Schuster, a professor of environmental studies at Humboldt University, to conclude, "All of this hot air must certainly have an effect on something."

This got some chuckles from the audience but groans from the panel of speakers.

The trash talk workshops were loud, animated, and seemed to be enjoyed by all. The camaraderie within the group was beyond what either environmentalist or athlete would have expected.

The sessions ended on time, and everyone headed to their hotel rooms to dress for the banquet.

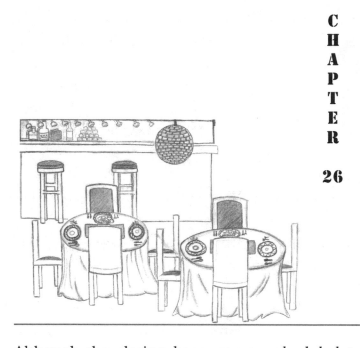

Although the closing banquet was scheduled to begin with cocktails at seven, Arnie and his committee members arrived at six to check out the Grand Ballroom. They were thrilled with what the hotel staff had accomplished. Three well-stocked bars were set up on different sides of the huge room. Twisted silver foil strands were hung from the ceiling and glistened as a large mirrored ball rotated near the ceiling in the center of the room and reflected the light from four spotlights shining on it from high on the ballroom walls. The light color changed at fifteen second intervals adding a surreal feel to the room. Enormous floral arrangements had been placed in each corner of the ballroom and each table had a beautiful bouquet on an elevated stand so it didn't prevent the guests at the table from seeing each other and being able to converse. On the one side of the room that lacked a bar, a long hors d'oeuvres table was set up and decorated although food had not been placed as yet.

"God," said Arnie, "it's beautiful. Can you believe we're at the closing banquet? After tonight and tomorrow's farewell breakfast it's over!"

"Yes," said Pam, "but I still can't believe we are really pulling it off."

"Oh man," Jordy chimed in. "By noon tomorrow I think I'll be in bed and spend a week there recovering. Hey Melissa, why are you so quiet?"

"I'm just in awe," said Melissa. "With all the problems and the giant misunderstanding, I still can't believe that everything seems to have worked. Everyone seems reasonably happy and the sessions certainly generated a lot of good discussion and interaction."

"Yeah," said Pam, "and we didn't have to quell a riot, although I thought that on registration day that is exactly what was going to happen."

"Yep," said Arnie, "I guess we lucked out. Maybe we're being rewarded from above for being such great people!"

They all laughed.

"Hey," said Arnie, let's break with our staid behavior and go over to the Boat House bar and have a pre-cocktail time drink."

"Good idea," said Jordy.

And the group headed out of the ballroom without noticing the back door open as three very large figures quietly entered the ballroom.

At five minutes to seven, the four committee members returned to the ballroom lobby where a fairly large number of meeting participants waited outside the closed ballroom doors. Arnie, fortified by his one martini, was in a jovial mood and loudly proclaimed, "For all of you overanxious party goers who have a large thirst and a grand appetite, I have come to save you and open the doors to the feast."

Amidst a cheer from the group, Arnie flung open the double doors at the main entrance, and he gasped.

"Holy shit," exclaimed Jordy as the crowd, about to enter, stopped.

"Oh my God," cried Pam, "we've been sabotaged!"

The sight they viewed was far different from an hour earlier. The bright rotating mirrored ornament was not rotating, and the spotlights were off. Instead, the room was dimly lit by red spotlights that flooded the room with a dim, eerie glow that made it difficult to clearly see in any great detail. But it was obvious that tables and floor were strewn with garbage. Chairs were overturned and even the bars and the hors d'oeuvres table were covered with what appeared to be pieces of fruit, tin cans, and other assorted debris.

Arnie was speechless and even felt tears well up in his eyes.

There was a silence among the group.

Even Rama Schriff, Arnie's boss, who had been anxious to come to the closing banquet, was stunned and once again, his Indian accent became exaggerated. "Oh my goodness gracious," he said softly, "this looks worse than a Calcutta back street. Oh my, I am thinking that I might just go over to the Boat House and have a calming libation. I know that you will handle this, Arnie. You are a good man." And he left, mumbling to himself, "Oh my goodness, Oh my goodness."

One of the environmentalists, a small woman from Philadelphia, burst into tears and sobs. "How could someone do such a terrible thing?" she wailed. "It must have been some right-wing anti-environmentalists."

"Maybe someone has a gripe against athletes," said a six foot seven basketball player.

Slowly, the crowd, led by Arnie, Pam, Melissa, and Jordy, began to move through the door into the dimly lit room.

Suddenly, bright lights came on and a group of about twenty people came rushing from the service area. At the same time people began to pop up from behind banquet tables, the bar, and the food table.

"Surprise!" they started shouting as they rushed out with plastic bags and plastic garbage cans and began retrieving the fake plastic garbage and trash that had been placed around the room.

Within a minute or two, as the stunned group of observers stood just inside the door, the whooping gang of athletes and environmentalists that had perpetrated the practical joke, led by Chuck Barkey, Sterling Parsche, and Bill Gladly, had removed all the "props," returned the lighting to normal, and the room looked as beautiful as it had when the committee had seen it earlier.

Chuck Barkey stepped forward facing the

entering crowd. "Welcome to our banquet. We thought that you would get a kick out of our little joke. Hey, Arnie, relax. Somebody better hold him up so he doesn't faint."

Gladly and Parsche ran over and held Arnie up.

Everyone laughed, but Arnie and his committee members were still breathing heavily as the mirrored ball began to rotate and a string quartet that had appeared in the back corner of the room began to play.

"Don't look so worried, Arnie," Parsche said. "We borrowed the garbage props from the Ringling Museum and some of us athletes pitched in for the quartet. So let's have a great time!"

The remaining crowd pushed into the ballroom and stormed the bars and the hors d'oeuvres table. Everyone was chattering about the prank and was in high spirits.

Arnie finally took a deep breath and began to laugh. He actually hugged Chuck Barkey although his head rested at Barkey's chest level. Everyone was happy.

At 8:00, the group took their seats for dinner, and Arnie went to a podium that was set up at the front of the room. Someone tapped their glass to draw attention to Arnie, and the group quieted.

Arnie began, "I know that we have our departure breakfast tomorrow morning, but since some of you have early flights and others may prefer to sleep in, I thought that I would make some remarks tonight. First, I can't thank you all enough for the wonderful participation at all the sessions and at the events. This is a meeting that I will never forget and I certainly think that goes for Pam, Jordy, and Melissa, as well. We particularly won't forget the garbage prank. I'm still shaking."

The crowd laughed. Mr. Mundhill, who was at a table near the front door with Mr. Schriff and some office employees, just shook his head slowly back and forth. No smile was apparent.

"I want to especially thank my three fellow committee members and also Chuck Barkey, Randy Wilson, Bernie McCann, and Max Gordon for joining our committee to redo the agenda after we became aware of the confusion about the meeting. I'm not going to go on with a long speech since dinner is being served, but I can say that I never believed the way this meeting started it could have turned out the way it did. I sincerely believe that everyone, environmentalists and athletes, learned a great deal. Thanks to all of you. Maybe we started a new tradition for future meetings. Enjoy your dinner and the rest of the evening."

As Arnie stepped away from the podium, several participants stood as everyone began to applaud and soon the entire group was giving Arnie a standing ovation. Mundhill was standing and Arnie thought he saw a clap or two. Arnie had tears in his eyes as he went to his table. He had never been so touched.

The dinner was a tremendous success and, although the departure breakfast was pretty well attended, the crowd was a bit subdued as they recovered from the previous night's festivities. Arnie stood by the dining room door along with Jordy, Pam, and Melissa, and they personally wished each departing attendee the best for the coming year and thanked them for their attendance.

Chuck Barkey, Too Fat McCann, Randy Wilson, and Max Gordon finished breakfast and were leaving together. As they got to the door, Barkey went to Arnie and gave him a big hug. This time Chuck bent his knees so they were closer to equal size. The rest of the group also hugged and shook hands and all were thanking each other for the exceptional efforts and the wonderful meeting.

"I'm gonna attend next year," said McCann, "but wherever it is don't let me near no water!"

They all laughed.

"I think I might attend next year too," said Wilson.

"Hey," exclaimed Barkey, "we all should attend. But Arnie, I got a favor to ask of you."

"What is it Chuck? Anything. I'll do it. I owe you."

"Okay, Arnie, once I get back to the Ritz I am going to find out where a special hotel trainee named Leona is going to be assigned next year. I'll let you know and I want you to use your influence to get the society to hold the meeting in that city. That shouldn't be a problem for someone as important as you."

"You got it buddy. Anything for you. Consider it done," said Arnie with his shoulders squared and his chest puffed out and they all laughed.

They had really done it. Arnie could hardly believe it. He, along with the other committee members, truly believed that everyone had benefited from the mixed audience. It was the best. And, thank God, it was over!

Arnie turned to see Mundhill and Schriff standing behind him. Mundhill had his suitcase in hand.

"Schwartz," he said, "I gotta hand it to you. You pulled it off. I'm not thrilled with all the hoopla and crap and in a way I still think I should fire your ass. But I suppose all's well that ends well. He turned and started to walk away and then turned back to say, "That goes for you too, Schriff," before continuing on.

Schriff called out, "Edmund," and Mundhill stopped and half turned back to face Schriff. "I hope that you learned some things this week, Edmund."

"Yeah?" said Mundhill.

But before he could say more, Rama Schriff continued, "Yes, you saw how much a well-managed, small office can accomplish."

Mundhill lowered his chin and raised his eyebrows over the top of his glasses, peering at Schriff.

Rama continued, "And Edmund, you should have learned that people of very different backgrounds and interests can appreciate each other and work together and learn from each other."

Mundhill slowly nodded his head. Then he turned and began to walk away as he said, "See you around, Schriff."

Mr. Schriff turned to Arnie. "Well, Arnie, we did it. I think now I will be taking my vacation. Perhaps a trip to Mumbai and Calcutta and Dehli. You take charge while I'm away.

Before Arnie could say a word, Mr. Schiff turned and was gone like the wind.

The following week Arnie and his coworkers were on a tremendous high. What a success. The *Sarasota Herald Tribune* even had a feature article on Sunday describing the meeting and how it evolved. The headline read: STRANGE BEDFELLOWS BENEFIT THE ENVIRONMENT. The article described the events leading to the initial confusion, the strange mix of attendees, and the actions to modify the agenda. It held high praise for the Sarasota Environmentalist chapter and particularly for Arnie and his committee. It also provided a highly positive picture of the role of the athletes and gave them a very complimentary review for interest beyond the world of sports.

This aspect of the article was picked up by several of the news syndicates and write-ups appeared in many newspapers and on several newscasts complimenting professional athletes beyond their sports accomplishments. The meeting even became a prime topic for radio talk show hosts and late night television. In addition, a couple of network news shows mentioned it.

One newspaper article summed it up, "Only time will tell whether the impact of this type of activity exhibits itself in any behavioral changes in our pro athletes."

SIX MONTHS LATER

An article appeared in the November 23 issue of the *New York Times* that was brought to Arnie's attention. He read it with great curiosity, and he really became choked up as he read.

About six months ago a little known meeting occurred in Sarasota, Florida. It's attendance and content were quickly and drastically changed at the last minute because of a fascinating mix-up. This was the National Environmentalist's annual meeting held this year under the sponsorship

of the small Sarasota branch of that
organization.

The article, which started on the front page
and continued in the sports section, detailed the
meeting, its original intent, the source of the confusion, the efforts to adjust the meeting and it described, in general, how the meeting progressed.
It went on to state:

Several newspaper articles that
appeared shortly after the meeting
provided a description and ended
with the thought: would there be
any impact on the behavior of pro
athletes as a result?

Well, this writer decided to explore that question now that six
months have elapsed. Some of my
findings are fascinating.

At a hockey game in Detroit,
where a strange custom has evolved
of throwing live octopii (octopuses)
on the ice after a Detroit goal, the
players are now picking them up
and placing them in a large aquar-
ium at one end of the rink so that

they can be returned to the sea. The Detroit public relations personnel claim that this bizarre behavior of the fans is now beginning to subside.

At Giants Stadium in New Jersey, New York Giant football players have been staying on the field for part of the halftime break and again after the game to pick up paper and other debris on the field. Reports claim that litter thrown onto the field has decreased.

Bud Salen, the commissioner of baseball, has rescinded the rule requiring that brooms, vacuums, and mops be kept at field side in case of emergencies. He claims that since May, the players' behavior has become so gentlemanly that the burden of extra emergency cleaning paraphernalia is unnecessary.

Then there was the story of Max Gordon, the Orlando basketball player who attended the Sarasota meeting, urging the non-starters on the Orlando team to sweep and polish the basketball court after each game and, as part of their daily exercise routine, to run through the stands picking up trash.

All in all, it seems like that little Sarasota meeting had some broad-reaching, very positive impact. And this writer has not seen any related negatives. Although, in a recent phone call to Arnie Schwartz, the chairperson of the May meeting, I asked him what he thought of the draft of this article that I sent him prior to publication. He said he thought it was great and if anyone didn't like it, and I quote Arnie, "Tell them to stick it where the sun won't burn a hole in the ozone layer."

I guess that trash talk is not dead. Here's to you, Arnie, and all your fellow environmentalists.